Published by Pink Tree Publishing Limited in 2023

All characters and events in this publication, other than those clearly in the public domain, are fictitious and any resemblance to real persons, living or dead, is purely coincidental.

Copyright © Pink Tree Publishing Limited.

The moral right of the author has been asserted.

All rights reserved. This book or any portion thereof
may not be reproduced or used in any manner whatsoever
without the express written permission of the publisher
except for the use of brief quotations in a book review.

For questions and comments about this book, please contact
pinktreepublishing@gmail.com

www.pinktreepublishing.com
www.agathafrost.com

WANT TO BE KEPT UP TO DATE WITH AGATHA FROST RELEASES? *SIGN UP THE FREE NEWSLETTER!*

www.AgathaFrost.com

You can also follow **Agatha Frost** across social media. Search 'Agatha Frost' on:

Facebook
Twitter
Goodreads
Instagram

ALSO BY AGATHA FROST

Claire's Candles
1. Vanilla Bean Vengeance
2. Black Cherry Betrayal
3. Coconut Milk Casualty
4. Rose Petal Revenge
5. Fresh Linen Fraud
6. Toffee Apple Torment
7. Candy Cane Conspiracies

Peridale Cafe
1. Pancakes and Corpses
2. Lemonade and Lies
3. Doughnuts and Deception
4. Chocolate Cake and Chaos
5. Shortbread and Sorrow
6. Espresso and Evil
7. Macarons and Mayhem
8. Fruit Cake and Fear
9. Birthday Cake and Bodies
10. Gingerbread and Ghosts

11. Cupcakes and Casualties
12. Blueberry Muffins and Misfortune
13. Ice Cream and Incidents
14. Champagne and Catastrophes
15. Wedding Cake and Woes
16. Red Velvet and Revenge
17. Vegetables and Vengeance
18. Cheesecake and Confusion
19. Brownies and Bloodshed
20. Cocktails and Cowardice
21. Profiteroles and Poison
22. Scones and Scandal
23. Raspberry Lemonade and Ruin
24. Popcorn and Panic
25. Marshmallows and Memories
26. Carrot Cake and Concern
27. Banana Bread and Betrayal

Other

The Agatha Frost Winter Anthology

Peridale Cafe Book 1-10

Peridale Cafe Book 11-20

Claire's Candles Book 1-3

1

"Hickory dickory dock..." Jessie muttered as she waved a buttered toast triangle with a bite missing through the line of Julia's distracted gaze. "Chill out and stop worrying."

Julia tore her eyes away from the clock on the wall of the café's kitchen and returned to the cake she'd been decorating. With the piping bag still in her grip, she gave the buttercream-fattened bag a twist and squeezed fluffy peaks around the edge of the freshly baked carrot cake. "I'm not worried."

"Liar." Jessie waved the toast again as Julia's eyes drifted. "The mouse ran up the clock..."

"Honestly," Julia said, this time with a more genuine smile, "I'm not worried."

"Tell that to your eyebrows."

Jessie imitated an exaggerated frown before she returned her attention to scrolling through whatever she was reading on her tablet. Julia let the tension she hadn't realised she'd been holding melt off her forehead, accepting that she was nervous while wishing she wasn't.

Jessie had never come to the closed café for breakfast before college on any other morning, but Julia was glad her daughter had picked today to stop in. She'd thought it was the café's new starter, Melissa, ready to start her first day when she heard the knock. Julia had been just as relieved to see Jessie, who never let anything get past her. Her daughter had been sneaking in pep talks since she'd sat down with her tablet.

Julia added a green and orange icing carrot to the centre of the smoothed buttercream surface. "I want things to go well, that's all. How does it look?"

Julia took a mouthful of the leftover buttercream from the piping bag before offering it to Jessie. She turned her nose up at it but accepted the tip anyway. Her eyes shot open in surprise.

"Mmm. Is that lemon?"

"Thought it would cut through the cinnamon a little." Julia bit her lip. For once, she hadn't trialled it. "Too much?"

"Delicious." Jessie squeezed out another length of

the buttercream Julia had worn her arm out whipping to its current state of fluffiness. "I'd say save me a slice, but it'll be sold out by lunchtime. And Melissa's still got five minutes to get here. Did you let her know we show up ten minutes before opening to ease in?"

Julia nodded as Jessie brushed the toast crumbs from her crinkled black Metallica T-shirt before sliding off her stool. Julia suddenly didn't want Jessie to go to college, but she followed her through the beaded curtain and into the café anyway. She slid the finished carrot cake into the middle of the revolving display case. The green and orange carrot creation shone as vibrant as the real thing behind the wall of mouth-watering peaks.

Julia's carrot cake was always a big seller in the spring, and she didn't doubt Jessie's prediction would come true, but she always had at least three backups ready for decorating in the fridge at all times.

"Don't you think she'd want to make a good impression on her first day?" Julia thought aloud, her eyes finding the café's clock on the wall among photographs of Peridale's countryside. "Or at least called if she's really late?"

"Those old work rules have gone out the window. I bet she'll turn up bang on the hour. Want me to stick around until she gets here?"

"No, no." Julia pushed forward a smile. "You get

yourself off to college. The whole point of hiring someone is so that the café doesn't interfere with your studies. What's your first class of the day?"

"English." Jessie sighed, and lines like the ones Julia imagined Jessie saw between *her* brows appeared on Jessie's much younger twenty-year-old face. "Don't suppose you remember much about *Romeo and Juliet*?"

Julia's stomach squirmed. She couldn't recall a thing outside the obvious stuff, and had it really been so many years that she'd forgotten the details? "Not unless you want the Leonardo DiCaprio version from 1996. Roxy dragged me to see it almost weekly when it first came out."

"You're so old."

"You're so sweet. And your dad's likelier to have an answer to your question. He's downstairs with a potential new client. Widow. Seemed distraught on the way in, but you might be able to catch him before you set off."

Jessie rocked back on her heels, knuckles whitening around the straps of her backpack—her turn to fixate on the clock. "Are you sure you don't want me to stay? We can get quite busy on Fridays."

Julia sensed her daughter's hesitation and hated that she couldn't offer more help with her college work. Though Julia could rustle up a recipe in no time and simple equations came easy to her, she hadn't been able to offer any help with Jessie's maths work. The science might as well have been brand new to her, too. She'd passed her exams with good grades, but it turned out that, at forty-one, her memory banks had refreshed a few too many times to remember the specifics of her high school lessons. "You don't work Fridays anymore, and I'm sure whatever you've written is great."

Jessie snorted. "I'm sure it's not. And I'm sure Melissa won't be like the other two. You said it yourself – she was enthusiastic when you told her the job was hers. She's probably just running a little late. See you later."

Jessie left with a jangle of the bell, and hoping she was right about not needing to worry, Julia dropped a peppermint and liquorice tea bag into a cup and watched as the clock ticked closer to eight. She'd arrived hours before she should have on her first day in the café all those years ago—a bundle of nerves and excitement. So many processes to learn. So many systems to figure out. It had been her dream for as long as she could remember, and she wasn't sure if she'd ever been as excited as she'd been on that first day.

Of course, she didn't expect the same level of enthusiasm from a teenager – not even Jessie matched Julia's passion – but she did expect people to arrive at work as close to on time as possible. Maybe nerves were keeping Melissa outside, just around the corner, terrified to come in?

Julia's own nerves had started in bed the night before, when faced with the idea of training her third new employee in as many months. She'd tossed and turned, much to her husband's grumbling. Like Jessie, Barker had assured her everything would go well when he'd been in the middle of flipping his pillow and noticed she was still awake.

In the light of the warm spring day, she knew it had been a waste of energy. She should have spent her time wondering if Melissa would even turn up.

"Julia?" The familiar voice of her gran, Dot, accompanied by rattling knuckles on the window in the door, snapped Julia back to the café. She flicked off the hot water tap, her teacup overflowing on the saucer. "It's one minute past the hour, Julia. Today is the new girl's first day, isn't it?"

Here's hoping, Julia thought, tugging the creases out of her apron as she headed to the door. Ready or not, it was another sunny spring day in Peridale, and it was Julia's job to be ready to serve the villagers, Melissa or no Melissa.

2

Explore how Shakespeare presents Juliet as a character who is determined in Romeo and Juliet *during Act Five, Scene Three, as well as the play as a whole.*

The mock exam question plagued Jessie like it had all week as she leaned against her yellow Mini Cooper in the shadowy alley between the café and the post office. *Why do they have to word things in a way that makes it sound like there's no wrong answer?*

And it wasn't even a question.

Explore.

Yeah, right.

Jessie might not have finished school the first time around, but when it came to education and exams, there was always a right answer and a wrong answer. She knew that, at least.

She strained her ears as footsteps made their way up the wooden stairs leading to the basement office under the café. If she set off in the next five minutes, she'd arrive at college just on time. Judging by how many rattles of the café bell she'd heard since she'd left, Melissa had missed her chance to do the same. Dot was gossiping about something on the other side of the wall, but even that wouldn't be enough to keep Julia distracted. Not by a long shot.

"And like I said," Jessie's dad's voice filled the yard behind the café, "I'd be happy to talk to you again at another time, Mrs Hardy."

Mrs Hardy, the widow in all black, kept her head down and her nose buried in a scrunched tissue as she swept past Jessie in a flurry of tears.

"Dare I ask?" Jessie popped her head through the open gate. Barker glanced over his shoulder with a more amused smile than she'd expected as he locked his door. "What did you say to her?"

"She seems to think *aliens* abducted her husband," Barker said, swinging the key around on his finger as he turned away from his black office door. "Only to return him, dead in bed next to her in an instant, with planted evidence that he'd died of a stroke."

"Why on Earth," she said, and immediately corrected to, "or *any* planet, would she think that?"

"Apparently, she saw a bright light," he said, spreading his hands out. "Brighter than any light she'd ever seen. Brighter than any light that exists on this planet."

"I assume she's verified that?"

"Poor woman ran off when I suggested she might have seen car headlights or maybe even a helicopter. Apparently, I'm 'just like the others' and, thus, not the PI for her. Grief works in mysterious ways, but the case would have been interesting."

"You'd have taken it?"

"Perhaps I could have helped her come to her senses by proving that he *did* die of a stroke. And it's not like I'm batting away new clients." Barker held his arms out at the empty field behind the café as though it were his office's waiting room. "But I'm not going to let that dampen things. Not today. The sun is shining, the birds are chirping, and I'm on my way to pick up my keys from the Council."

"Keys for what?"

"My very own allotment." He rubbed his hands together, his gaze far off. "This day has been a long time coming."

Jessie bit back her grin as Barker stared far off into the distance, like an adventurer about to set off on the treasure hunt of a lifetime. She'd never heard her dad mention anything about an allotment before.

"Shouldn't you be at college?" He wriggled back his sleeve and checked his watch, already on his way down the alley. "Did you want me for something?"

Jessie's grip squeezed around her bag straps, knowing she wouldn't pull her tablet out to show him. Her no-doubt-terrible analysis of a Shakespeare play she could barely wrap her head around would be enough to ruin anyone's morning. Besides, if it was as bad as she feared, a five-minute scan in the alley wouldn't help.

"Just wanted to see what the widow was about," she said, pulling out her car keys. Her Mini chirped a light-flashing greeting. "I'll keep an eye on the skies for flying saucers."

"Let me know if you see any little green men. I'll send you a picture of the allotment when I get there. Have a good day."

"Have a good ... allotment."

Behind the wheel of her car, she pulled out her tablet and scrolled to the top of the document. What would another ten minutes matter? As she read her own words for the millionth time, she tried to remember why she'd thought education would be any easier this time.

Because she was older?

Good one.

She hadn't understood Shakespeare at sixteen and didn't understand him at twenty, and it was taking all her willpower not to throw her tablet into the field in exchange for the comfort of her café apron.

With his fingers turning the allotment key over in his pocket as he rounded the corner at the top of Mulberry Lane, Barker tried to remember the man he'd been when he'd first driven into Peridale in a half-empty moving van.

Long before his life in Peridale with Julia, the girls, the office, and the trouble-seeking grandmother-in-law, Barker had been sure he'd peaked. He'd been propelled through the police ranks from the moment he'd passed his exams with flying colours, and by his early thirties, he thought he had everything he ever wanted.

An apartment with a city view, a job with status, and even a fiancée, Vanessa. And then Vanessa, a lovely police constable, was killed. Murdered. Shot by a madman seeking revenge for a drunk driving conviction that had 'ruined his life.' Vanessa hadn't even been the officer to arrest him. His revenge destroyed Barker's completed life, and he often wondered who he'd be if another officer had answered the call.

Married to Vanessa? Looking back, he'd hardly known her. He'd loved her, but he knew it was a naive love compared to what he and Julia shared. Still, maybe they'd have made it. They'd have moved to a penthouse, and he'd have risen all the way to the top of the ranks and retired with a chest glittering with badges and medals.

It took him too many years of limping along in the city to realise that dream had died with Vanessa. After spending one too many nights staring out at the city, alone in his bed, reading a murder mystery set in a small rural village was the spark that lit the match that led him to request a transfer.

"Anywhere rural," he'd said.

Peridale might as well have been plucked out of a hat.

Though the author of the mystery had described a place of gossipy neighbours always peeking through the curtains and a scandal waiting around every corner, Barker had seen the peace and quiet between the lines. As it turned out, the author hadn't been far off.

But not today.

Not even widows and aliens could distract from his excitement.

Hurrying past the pink glow of Katie's Salon in the middle of Peridale's main shopping street, Barker pulled out his wallet and peeled back the tiny leather sleeve behind his bankcards. He plucked out the bar napkin he'd pulled from under his whisky to scribble his 'Before Forty' plan on with a pen borrowed from the bartender.

Leave city.
Move to a village.
Retire.
Write book.
Get allotment.
Live out days peacefully.

Barker had written the list in chronological order of when he thought he'd achieve them, yet all but 'get allotment' and 'live out days peacefully' had been ticked off.

Julia's father, who ran the antiques shop in the barn at the bottom of the street, waved to Barker. Thankfully, he was busy trying to sell someone an iron sewing machine attached to its own wooden table. Barker returned the wave and sped up. Ducking and weaving along a narrow path running alongside the abandoned builder's yard, Barker checked the handwritten instructions the man at the Council had given him.

"'Turn left at bottom of Mulberry Lane, carry on to

the sign, left at the big tree, and it's just down the way,'" he read aloud. "Just down the way?"

Barker reached a fork in the path, and found a sign for the Howarth walking trail pointing in one direction; a sign for Riverswick in the other; and another, for Peridale, pointing back the way he'd come.

"Are you lost, ma'love?" A gruff, warm voice came from his left, catching Barker off-guard. "Because you looks a little lost to me."

A stout woman with eyes as green as the leaves of the plants bobbing up and down in her wheelbarrow peered up at him from underneath a mop of thick grey curls crammed under a brown bucket hat. Her knees and fingers were caked in mud, and she even had a little smudge of it on the end of her nose above her grin. Staring into her catlike eyes reminded Barker of waking up with Mowgli purring on his chest and clawing at his chin.

"I'm heading to the allotment," he said, pointing in the direction at which her wheelbarrow was aimed. "This way?"

"Aye, this way." She trundled down the path, following the sign leading to Riverswick, and Barker hurried to keep up – she was light on her feet. "You're not one of them property developers, are you? Because if you are, I'll whack you with my shovel."

Her voice held no trace of humour, and she did, in fact, have a shovel in her wheelbarrow. Barker chuckled, though he hadn't been a retired Detective Inspector for that long. *Wits about you, Brown*, he reminded himself. *You're in the middle of nowhere with a stranger, sweet old lady or not.*

"I'm not a property developer," he said, catching up. He decided 'private investigator' might rattle her in a different way. "I've just been given the keys to an allotment."

The woman stopped and let the wheelbarrow fall. The plants rustled as she spun around and lifted her curly fringe and the brim of her hat to stare up at Barker with wide eyes.

"Give over!" She forced a belly laugh as she planted her balled-up hands on her middle. "Bit young, aren't you? When did you put your name on the waiting list?"

"About four years ago," he said, pulling out the letter he'd received yesterday but only got around to opening that morning over breakfast. "I put my name down when I first moved to the village, and I guess it's my turn."

"Four years?" She laughed again. "*Four*? Kevin waited nine, and Martha for twelve! Getting a Council allotment is an honour, so you should count yourself lucky. Name's Coral, by the way." Coral dusted her hand down her tatty cardigan and outstretched it to Barker. "Bit of mud surely can't scare you, can it? You do have gardening experience, I assume?"

Not realising he'd hesitated, Barker accepted her handshake while he weighed whether cutting the grass and yanking up weeds near the path when he saw them counted. "Some," he opted for, "and I'm Barker."

"Well, it's nice to meet you, Barker." Coral hoisted up the wheelbarrow with a grunt, steadied her grip, and set off marching as quickly as the spring breeze blew around them. "As I said, you're lucky. And you might be the youngest face on the block by a decade, at least. Once people have them, you usually have to wait until they die before they come up again. Unless someone moves away. What plot did you say you were in?"

"I didn't." He checked the red tag dangling from the bronze key. "Seven."

"Oh." She slowed down in the shadow of a tall oak tree twisted around a mound of earth that looked like it could crumble at any moment. "That'll be Tommy's plot. He used to come up quite regularly, but then his Leslie died, and well, he was never the same ..." Coral let her words drift before clearing her throat. "Did they say what happened to him?"

"Afraid not."

Coral grumbled, turning left at the big oak tree.

"It's just down the way," she called, speeding up so quickly along the bumpy gravel path that Barker didn't want to risk his knees trying to keep pace. "Plot Seven's right in the middle. You can't miss it. I'm two doors down, so I'll see you around."

"I'll see you" – Coral vanished out of sight – "around."

Barker couldn't think about his intriguing two-doors-down allotment neighbour for too long. The path curved and steepened before taking Barker further into the valley on a curved downward that he assumed must be 'just down the way.'

No sign marked the entrance to the allotment, just a mural graffitied on the side of a pebble-dashed electricity building. A shade-wearing sun beamed out over beds of flourishing vegetables on a day as pleasant as the one they were currently having. Beyond the mural, a single path split the rows of allotments into two. Cobbled together from bits of scrap as it was, the place wasn't much to look at, but Barker was sure he'd be as happy as the sun in the shades soon – if only he'd brought his sunglasses too.

A metal gate that looked as though it had been scavenged from an industrial estate swung inwards after he unlocked Plot Seven using one of the keys. Four overgrown beds greeted him, fenced in with wooden slatted fences on both sides and sheets of corrugated metal running along the back wall. Mud-caked tools filled one corner, a shed the other.

It was a mess.

It was now Barker's mess.

And he had no idea where to start.

He had all the time in the world to learn how to grow carrots, potatoes, and tomatoes. But first, he had eyes on something that poked out of the overgrown vegetable patch at the back of the allotment. Shielding his eyes from the bright sun, the author within him tried to figure out if he was really seeing a shoe, or if it was just a trick of his imagination.

3

"Julia, I *have* to ask," Evelyn, the local bed and breakfast owner and Julia's first paying customer of the morning, remarked as she swirled her teacup around. "What *are* you doing?"

Julia was distracting herself from the fact that she was an hour into her shift at the café with no sight or sound of her new employee, but she knew that wasn't what Evelyn meant.

"You ask an awful lot of questions for someone who claims to be psychic." Dot's faux-under-her-breath mutter rang out with only the three of them in the café, not that Evelyn's smile wavered as she watched Julia pluck another egg from the basket. Dot peered over the table and, less politely, asked, "But yes, Julia, *what* are you doing?"

Crouching next to her gran's table, Julia grabbed a foil-wrapped chocolate egg from the wicker basket, snapped off a length of tape from a packing roll, and slapped it under the table. Even in her eighties, Julia's gran was limber enough to wrap her head halfway around the underside of the table. Her pruned lips pointed at Julia as she pressed the air bubbles from the tape.

"If I had to guess," Evelyn said brightly as she pressed her fingers to the sides of her turban. This morning, she'd opted for a springtime yellow with an airy kaftan to match. She closed her eyes and focused, while Dot became interested in checking her nails. "I'd say you were performing some kind of ritual."

"A ritual?" Dot flicked away whatever she'd picked out from under her thumbnail. "Like a cult? You think Julia has joined a cult?"

"Some sort of Easter ritual?" Clicking her fingers, Evelyn pulled the idea from thin air. "An offering. To…" Again, she snapped her fingers. "To…"

"The Easter Bunny?" Dot offered sardonically.

"Judging by the pattern of the tables you're taping eggs under, perhaps something pagan?" Evelyn shook her head at the suggestion as her fingers drummed on her chin. "No, I'd know if that was the case. Hmm."

Julia secured the final foil egg under the table closest to the door, chosen at random rather than for ritualistic reasons.

"Well, Julia?" Dot demanded, her voice coming from the counter. "What's with the eggs? Trying to summon the Easter bunny so you can sacrifice your soul for as many Easter eggs as you could possibly eat, as Evelyn suggested?"

"That's not *quite* what I said."

"Like most things around here, the truth is often a lot simpler," Julia said, shimmying around the revolving cake display case before dropping the basket under the counter. She grabbed a pot for her gran's inevitable second order on her way up. "Olivia's nursery has organised an Easter egg hunt around the village for Easter Sunday next week, and the route goes right across the green, past the café, to the church for the spring fete. They wanted some places indoors in case of rain, so I volunteered. Wanted to see if this tape was strong enough to keep them stuck up."

"I suppose it's the right height for toddlers," Dot mused, looking away from the cakes revolving under the spotlights to glance at the clock. "An hour late? Really? Where did you find *this* one?"

"It's not like I've been flooded with applications. Maybe her bus is running late? She seemed excited to start when I let her know she'd got the job, so I imagine there's a simple explanation."

"The simple explanation is that she's from a lazy generation," Dot declared, tapping the glass with her nail. "They don't want to do anything but sit around doing whatever it is they do these days."

"Let's be honest, Dot. People have been saying that for generations about every generation that follows. *Your* generation said that about *my* generation too."

"Yes, and maybe we weren't wrong." Dot shot Evelyn a glance hidden behind a smile. "And I'm not much older than you, dear. What's twenty years between friends?"

"Thirty, at least."

"I'll have a slice of the carrot cake when you're ready, Julia," Dot said, ignoring the correction. "Like I was saying, back in my day, we were grafters."

"And how was life as a chimney sweep, Gran?"

"My point being," Dot continued, following Julia to the till, "when *I* was this new girl's age, *I* wouldn't have dared turn up to work late, especially on *my* first day. I worked in a little theatre over on the other side of Riverswick. Gone now, but even though I was only taking the coats, I still treated the role very seriously. And I'm sure I was early on my first day. It's where I met your grandfather, you know. God rest his soul."

"Ever thought about past life regression, Dot?" Evelyn offered, joining them at the counter. "To see if you actually *were* a chimney—"

"No." The answer came out quickly, and Dot let the echo sit. "And rip open one of those teabags and ask the stars or spirits or wherever you get your information from? I'm sure someone out there in the ether must know what's holding Miss Melissa up, if it's not her own bone-idleness."

Evelyn reached into her kaftan rather than the teapot and pulled out her phone. She tapped, scrolled, and turned the screen.

"There's a protest outside the hospital that's got the morning traffic backed up all the way to the bypass near the farm up by Julia's," Evelyn said, as they both leaned in to look at the pictures. "Not quite the tea leaves, but people have been posting about it all morning. Seems to have ruined quite a few morning commutes."

"Protest?" Dot spun around, never one to miss the opportunity to pull out her megaphone. "What's the cause?"

"I'm not sure, but it's at the hospital." Evelyn tucked her phone away with a jangle of her beaded bracelets. "There were buses in that jam. Your new employee might be aboard, like you said, Julia."

Julia offered Evelyn a grateful smile. "Here's hoping."

"It's not like they have to run to the nearest phone box to let you know they're running late," Dot said, half under her breath again. "They don't know they're born. If she does turn up, you should fire her on the spot."

"I'll give her the benefit of the doubt," Julia said, accepting Evelyn's tray over the top of the coffee machine. "Evelyn's probably right. She'll be in the protest traffic. She loved the café. Said she loved the 'vibe' and couldn't wait to work here."

"It *does* have a nice aura," Evelyn said, giving Dot an up-and-down glance, "*most* of the time."

"Whatever happens," Dot said as Evelyn's comment clearly went over her head and Julia braced herself for what she knew was coming, "I'm sure she can't be any worse than the *last* one."

Julia glanced at Evelyn, hoping she'd moved on from the Nick incident, but the B&B owner's lips were already curling into the familiar apologetic smile. "I really am sorry about what happened with Nick."

"It's fine," Julia repeated. "He will have calmed down by now."

"Poor lad was just so interested in my tarot cards as I was shuffling them," she continued, her face darkening to a shade of red that made her yellow ensemble glow like a buttercup. "If I'd have known I'd pull the death card first, I wouldn't have offered to give him that free reading."

"You weren't to know his granddad was about to have that stroke."

"And despite what Nick thinks," Dot said, patting Evelyn's shoulder, "you probably didn't cause it."

"The universe does work in mysterious ways." Evelyn gave a shaky laugh as she fluttered away to the door in a haze of yellow chiffon. "I think I'll pop by the nursery and see if it's not too late to add my B&B to the route. Such a lovely idea."

The door closed behind Evelyn, but Dot's smile, with its wicked corners, didn't fade. Grandmother and granddaughter alike were amused by the mystic B&B owner, but in different ways. Julia hoped Evelyn meant it when she said she'd refrain from offering to take her new employees across the threshold into the spiritual realm ... at least until they'd got through their trials.

At this rate, anyone would be lucky to get that far.

"Poor boy was screaming on the phone like he'd been cursed by one of the Pendle witches themselves," Julia admitted in a whisper. "I can't help but think she did me a favour. He was sweet enough, but he wasn't picking up the rhythm of the place, and he couldn't get over his shyness to take orders."

"If only what's-her-face had been shyer." Dot's eyes rolled in their sockets. "Saskia. The 'singer' slash 'actress' slash 'model' who was only working here until her big break, and boy oh boy, would that girl not stop reminding you about it."

"To her credit, she *was* cast in that play."

"I'd hardly call a six-week stint in panto down in Brighton a 'big break,' but good luck to her, I say. I could have been an actress, you know." Dot drifted off for a moment, and Julia wondered if she was about to hear the story of how Dot met plumber, Albert, after a burst pipe in the theatre cloakroom, but a shake of her head brought her back to the present topic. "Anyway, I'll take this slice back to Percy and the dogs, since she's not turned up. We're out litter-picking at the top of the hour, then we have our 'movement' classes at the village hall, and then it's bingo over in Oxford."

"Quite the busy day."

Dot grumbled deep in her throat. Ignoring the tightest purse of her grandmother's lips all morning, Julia wrapped the cake in waxpaper before pouring the tea into a cardboard cup.

"Percy's keeping me rather busy," Dot stated when

Julia left the bait lingering. "Insists it's what we need to do to stave off the boredom."

"Movement and bingo sound fun, Gran."

"*You* try spending your afternoon swinging your arms around before dabbing numbers on a sheet every Friday for two months, and we'll see if you're still jumping for joy. I need something more stimulating. I'm not dead yet, you know."

"Nobody is trying to put you out to pasture."

Julia waited for the conversation to nosedive right into 'well, if we were still running the neighbourhood watch group, I wouldn't be so bored' that usually followed Dot's recent declarations regarding the current status of her mortality, but her gran accepted her order and stepped back.

"One last thing before I go," she said while Julia scrolled to Melissa's name in her phone. "When did you last talk to your sister?"

"A few days ago. She asked if I could pick up the twins from nursery. Why?"

"And how'd she seem?"

"I didn't see her."

"Hmm, not just me, then." Dot's eyes went about the empty café before she leaned in. "I haven't seen her for easily a month. She's always too busy. As disgruntled as I am that she can't make time for her grandmother," Dot said, pausing the adjust the brooch at her collar, "I don't quite believe her when she says she's 'fine,' and that's only when I manage to catch her on the phone for more than a few seconds. I know what she's like. *You* know what she's like. Can you check up on her?"

"Already on it," Julia said, her thumbs working on her keyboard, having switched 'Melissa' for 'Sue.' "I'll see if she's working tonight. She could be stressed from the house move? Everything was so last minute."

"Perhaps," Dot agreed with a nod, "but you and I both know what's been going on with Sue has been going on longer than that."

Julia's gut writhed, knowing what her gran was hinting at. She'd been watching her little sister sprinting behind her for a while, but Sue never grabbed hold whenever Julia held out a hand to pull her up. The phone in her hand pinged, and she half-expected to see her sister's name on the screen, but despite what Evelyn thought, the universe didn't work that strangely.

One new text message from Melissa: *Sorry. Sick. Can't make it.*

As simple as the explanation was, Julia would have preferred if it had arrived before she'd flipped the sign for the day. But, like she'd told her gran, she'd give Melissa the benefit of the doubt. Everyone deserved a second chance, even if Julia felt her own 'back in my day' rant brewing at the tips of her fingertips as they hovered above the keyboard to reply. She opted for 'Hope you feel better soon, and if you do, I'll see you on Monday for your next shift.' before pushing forward her brightest smile as the bell announced that she wasn't alone.

"Have you heard?" Roxy Carter, one of Julia's closest friends, called into the empty café. Julia's smile dropped at her panicked tone. From the looks of it, Roxy had her entire Year Six class behind her.

"What's happened?"

"We were on a school outing to the allotment to find and document flora and fauna," Roxy said, leaning in as a shaky smile rattled her cheeks and contradicted the harrowed look in her eyes. "Taken weeks to plan a school trip to take them ten minutes around the corner, so of course, it's all gone backside up. We couldn't even get to the bottom of Mulberry Lane. The whole place is closed off." Even lower, she added, "I heard someone outside Vicky's Coffee Van say they found a body, and you're never going to guess in whose allotment."

"Haven't been over that way since we were kids. I don't think I even know anyone with an allotment."

The piece of tape she'd stuck under the table nearest the door crackled away from the wood, and a pink foil egg cracked against the floorboards, but Julia couldn't bring herself to look away from Roxy's gaze. She'd known her best friend long enough to know that she knew something Julia didn't.

"Rox?"

"You might want to talk to your husband, because it turns out you *do* know someone with an allotment."

4

Jessie's eccentric English tutor, Veronica Hilt, stood at the head of the classroom, trying her best to keep everyone engaged in the final minutes of the lesson with her usual flapping arms and theatrical delivery. Given how many faces were glowing from the phones tucked under desks, Jessie was the only one still listening. At least, trying to. Jessie had never met anyone who talked faster than Veronica.

A yawn fluttered her lips, but she wasn't the only one who'd been yawning all lesson. How many others had stayed up late scratching their heads over the mock exam question? Of the ten students in the class, at least three hadn't handed anything in, and they'd been given an extension. If she'd known that would be an option, she'd have spent an extra day with it – not that she believed twenty-four hours would get her anywhere closer to her exploration being the right one.

She'd messed up.

While they'd been working on a creative writing task halfway through the day's lesson, Veronica tried to suppress a laugh that burst through her lips like a trumpet. They'd all laughed at the interruption, and Veronica apologised and told them to settle. Jessie's eyes lingered a little too long on her teacher's desk, and she recognised her work by the size she'd made the font before printing it off in the library. She'd been thirty minutes late in the end, but Veronica Hilt had strolled in ten minutes later behind sunglasses, with a Starbucks cup in hand and projecting a 'don't ask' air.

Veronica Hilt was nothing like any of the teachers Jessie remembered from the countless schools the foster system had dragged her through.

Jessie actually liked her, for a start. Veronica wore the brightest clothes Jessie had ever seen, but it was her collection of gigantic glasses that drew the most notice. She seemed to have a new pair every time Jessie saw her. Today, she'd gone for round red specs that reminded Jessie of Percy's, only quadruple the circumference.

"Right, that's a wrap for today," Veronica called

out, drumming her hands on the desk, and startling the students who'd tuned out long ago. "Always my favourite part of the lesson, seeing how many of you were actually paying attention. You know, you're not obliged to be here. In fact, you're all paying for the pleasure, so the joke's really on you." Her volume rose as the class emptied, but she didn't stand in anyone's way to leave. "Why don't you stay at home in your pyjamas the next time you want to spend an hour swiping through girls on dating apps, Ben?"

"I might just do that, Miss." Ben, one of the recent school leavers who'd spun right back through the swinging doors to try again after failing his exams, sucked the air in an attempt at being threatening. "This class is proper crap, anyway."

"Please, take up my offer," Veronica called through cupped hands. "But I'll see you on Tuesday, and don't forget your coursework this time."

"Or what, Miss?"

"I'll give you detention."

"You can't do that, Miss. We're not in school anymore."

"Exactly, so why do you keep calling me 'Miss' every other word? It's Veronica, and if you don't mind, I'd like to have a word with *Miss* Jessika here."

Hearing her full name caught Jessie off-guard. Not even Julia called her Jessika, but Veronica used it exclusively. Jessie stopped her slow shuffle down the aisle of tables and chairs as the last of her classmates, heads buried in their phones, drifted to the exit for their lunch break. Jessie wanted nothing more than to follow them – not that she'd made friends with any of them yet. Nor had they with each other, by the looks of it. Half were like Ben, fresh from high school, and the other half were in their thirties and older, all the way to a man sitting his GCSEs in his sixties – closer to Veronica's age. All of them had one thing in common – they wanted to get in and get out. It hadn't been the same on her catering course, but that had lasted a year. Here, they were already three months into their six-month short course.

"I hope you know what I'm going to say," Veronica said, leaning back in her chair and kicking her feet up on the desk. She pulled a satsuma from the pocket of her long red cardigan and began peeling it, which explained why Jessie's work always came back smelling zesty.

"That my work was so good they've had to invent a new grade to award me for my talents?"

"If I were awarding you for your humour, you'd score top marks. Class clown back when you were at school, were you?" Veronica peered over her glasses. "As I said, it's your choice to come here. I can tell you tried, at least, but I think you can do better than this."

Veronica plucked Jessie's work from the pile and brushed it across the desk with one hand while she continued peeling the satsuma in the other, rolling the fruit around in her palm like a trick she'd perfected decades ago. "Though your closing statement did make me laugh."

"I heard. Everyone heard. That bad?"

"No, it was funny." After all the peeling, Veronica bit into the satsuma like anyone else would an apple. "I think your observation that Juliet was determined to get herself killed 'for the first boy who batted lashes at her' is how many people your age would see it these days, but I know you've got a better head on your shoulders than that. I think you've missed the point of the text, so I'm giving you another chance to prove that you can get it. If you go back with fresh eyes and draw conclusions the exam board might be happy with, I'll regrade you."

"Was it really the worst?"

"I didn't say it was the worst." Veronica laughed, letting her feet fall to the floor before motioning to the empty classroom. "Not by a stretch. But like I said, I know you're better than that, so try again. And if you're going to make me laugh, back it up with something from the text."

Jessie slid her work off the desk, and her eyes glazed over at the sea of purple squiggles smothering the black text. Veronica never used red, but Jessie received the message loud and clear.

"I'll give it another go. Am I free to leave?"

"Like I said, Jessie, this is college. You're free to tell me to stick my advice where the sun doesn't shine, if you'd like." Veronica pulled a paperback book from her linen bag and thumbed it to the middle. "Now, if you don't mind, they barely give us breaks in this bloody place, and I want to find out how Poirot gets out of this one."

Leaving Veronica Hilt to point her giant specs at her pages of Poirot, Jessie set off in the direction of the canteen. The first hint of Ben's obnoxious voice swerved her down the staircase instead.

"And her head is shaped like a pigeon's." Ben's voice shrank as Jessie headed in the opposite direction. "Don't you all think she looks like a pigeon with big glasses? If she were my mum, I'd be well ashamed, man. Pigeon-head with glasses on."

Jessie sped up, unsure if she could cringe any harder than at Ben's third attempt to raise a laugh from 'pigeon-head.' Though she hated to admit it, the observation wasn't far off. Already pulling her copy of *Romeo and Juliet* from her bag, she strode into the Happy Bean coffee shop tucked away in a corner underneath the library.

She exhaled, glad to have escaped the noise,

although walking into Happy Bean always felt like a betrayal. The corporation's attempt to open a franchise in the village, directly on the doorstep of Julia's café, had backfired during Jessie's first year working there. Like Richie's, the bar that now occupied the site of the failed franchise, this particular Happy Bean had gone with the industrial brick-and-filament-light décor Jessie had seen in every corner of the world on her travels. Somehow, it was like walking onto a carefully designed television set that felt strangely familiar.

At least it was quiet.

Taking a sip of her caramel macchiato – watered-down swill compared to the strong stuff she made herself at Julia's – Jessie cracked open the stiff red fabric cover of the hardback, intending to spend the half an hour before double science giving the work her freshest eyes.

Eyes so fresh, it would be like she'd never read it before.

Except she had, several times, and she'd watched the weird 90s version on DVD when she still lived at the cottage with her mum and dad. Everyone knew what happened in Act Five, Scene Three, which she apparently still 'didn't get.' *What is there to get? Juliet finds Romeo dead, Juliet kills herself, and I'm supposed to believe it's the greatest love story ever told.*

A cautionary tale, more like.

No sooner had her eyes attuned to the strange rhythm of Shakespeare, Jessie spotted someone ducking to catch her attention. Wincing at the thought of it being Ben trying to hit on her again, she kept reading, but the distraction only moved closer. She looked up, prepared to have words with Ben, only to lock eyes with one of the last people she'd ever expect to see ... not only in the college, but anywhere near Peridale.

"Johnny?" Jessie immediately shut her book and smiled an apology for ignoring him so long. "Can't stay away from the place? We only watched you and Leah drive away from the village to start your new life last week. It's not all fallen apart already, has it?"

"You sound like my mother." Johnny glanced at the free chair across from her, and Jessie gestured towards it with a hand. He sat, yanking his messenger bag over his curly hair. "And unlike you, I know she's not joking. But no, there's no trouble in paradise. We're still settling into the new apartment, and Leah's house across from the street from your mum has almost sold, but ... you don't want to hear about that." He offered a nervous laugh and glanced at the book. His eyes lit up. "Shakespeare. How are you finding it?"

"Shakespeare? Or the college?"

"Both?"

Johnny Watson, the former editor of *The Peridale Post* and a long-time close friend of her mum's, had been one of the people to nudge her to give education another go. Jessie had even applied to college at his wedding to Leah Watson, formerly Burns – another of her mum's school friends. Jessie had ended the night full of hope that things would be different this time.

No matter how many times Veronica Hilt kept pointing out that things were different at college, some things stayed the same.

"Sort of feel like I might be messing the whole thing up," Jessie admitted, her throat clenching around the words as she let them out for the first time. "I just got a D on an English mock exam question. Might as well give up."

"Now, would Romeo and Juliet have given up if they'd thought like that?"

"They'd be alive."

Johnny laughed and fiddled with his glasses. "Good point. Shakespeare can be tricky."

"Did you ever get a D?"

"No." According to Roxy, Johnny had been the 'school swat,' so Jessie wasn't surprised. "But I know your mum used to struggle, and I used to help her with her Shakespeare coursework. I can't imagine much has changed. Do you want me to give you some pointers?"

"Really?" Jessie considered the offer, but a question brewed in place of her acceptance. "Wait, you didn't say what you were doing back here. I know you wanted a low-key move so you wouldn't feel like it was such a big deal when you popped back, but I wasn't expecting to see you so soon."

Johnny exhaled and looked around the nearly empty coffee shop. He leaned in and said, "The editor the paper hired to replace me left on his first day. Apparently, they felt the job was 'misrepresented,' so the paper has paid me to come back and find someone else. It took me long enough to find the first one. Leah's at a wedding fair, scouting for new suppliers anyway, so I'm staying at the house for the week to see if I can rustle something up before I start my new job. That's why I'm at the college. I interviewed a few tutors looking for new paths, but I'm not sure it was worth my time."

"What happens if you don't find anyone?"

Johnny inhaled. "It won't be my problem by then. Not that I blame anyone who doesn't want the job. There's not much to take over." He shook his head. "But enough about paper politics. I meant what I said if you need help with the English work. Cool edition, by the way. The college has stepped things up."

"Mum and Dad bought me a fancy set," she said,

running her fingers over the thick gold lettering embossed on the front. "They want me to do well."

"And you will." Johnny frowned into his lap before pulling up his phone. "I – I need to go. And here I was, thinking I'd have nothing to fill my last issue. Never a quiet day around here, eh?"

Johnny vanished as quickly as he'd arrived, and though Jessie wanted to get back to her book, she couldn't bring herself to lift the cover. Her parents had seemed so proud when they'd gifted her the set; like Johnny, they'd been certain she'd do well.

Everyone was sure, yet Jessie hadn't achieved above a C in anything. *Why am I here?* Draining her macchiato, she let the question rattle in her head. Speeding away in her Mini before double science started grew more attractive. She could be back at the café, getting to know Melissa the newbie, in no time.

Her phone vibrated in her backpack, and she wriggled it out, glad to be yanked out of the familiar spiral she'd been slipping into.

New image received from Dad: *So, about the allotment...*

Jessie whirled the dregs of her coffee around in the cup while she waited for the picture to load.

The image loaded, giving Jessie a view of her dad's new allotment, albeit from the other side of a police cordon. Without needing another excuse, Jessie stuffed the book into her bag and sprinted for the stairs, her car key already in hand.

What was it Johnny had said?

Never a quiet day in Peridale, and the vague text from Barker was loud enough to call her home.

Standing behind crime scene tape while a crew of retired villagers glared at Barker wasn't how he'd expected to spend his afternoon, but he'd lost control of that when he found the boot.

And, more importantly, the foot connected to the boot.

Barker had seen his fair share of corpses. Succumbing to the numbness that came with constantly being presented with death was easy, but DIs needed to put horrors to one side to deal with the scene before them.

The victim, possibly in his early thirties, judging by his receding hairline and lines around his eyes, had been buried in the carrots. Judging by how quickly carrots started to turn black at the cottage, these looked like they'd have been ripe for picking about a fortnight ago.

Given the body's peeled-back lips, lack of vigour,

and the insects already starting to return it to the ground, he'd also guess the same about the corpse.

Male.

White.

About five feet and ten inches, judging by the length of the beds, which he'd estimated to be six feet long by three wide. Plenty of space to bury a body, and yet Barker had clearly seen clothing poking through the soil. The victim's brown canvas jacket and green cotton V-neck shirt wouldn't have been out of place amongst the irritated gardeners whispering behind Barker.

Let them whisper. Barker could barely hear them anyway. Nothing woke the DI part of his brain faster than a fresh crime scene. But he wasn't a DI anymore, and if he were, he'd have any civilian who tried to duck under his cordon arrested, retired DI or not. He didn't know who was on the case yet – whomever they'd brought in hadn't left Plot Seven since their arrival behind the forensic crew.

Barker had been trying to catch the eyes of anyone, but the faces didn't match the ones he remembered—not that he could tell them apart. He'd never understood how people could say that all police officers looked the same until he left the force. Besides, he'd checked the map on his phone, and they'd technically crossed into Riverswick's jurisdiction somewhere around 'just down the way.'

He scanned the group for Coral, the only face that would be familiar to him, but she wasn't in the crowd. A flask of tea was being passed around, and they'd found logs and buckets to perch on, though they hadn't stopped shooting daggers in Barker's direction. If they were expecting an apology, they wouldn't get one. He hadn't planted the body with the carrots.

"Barker Brown?"

The excited whisper came from behind the cordon. Barker plastered his smile from ear to ear as his short-lived publicist had taught him. Since his mother had long since gone, there was only one reason someone would be using his full name – the same reason he'd had a publicist. He'd take the bright sun of a countryside lane, crime scene or not, over the bright studio lights of the daytime TV shows for which he'd learned the clown-like grin. He would have felt silly doing it if everyone else hadn't been, but it always worked.

"I *knew* it was you," said a young officer who looked too young to have earned his police constable badge already, but Barker didn't let the grin falter. "We've met before."

The PC hadn't mentioned Barker's book, *The Body in the Basement*, but his smile was the same adoring one Barker had seen from behind his share of signing desks. The officer had definitely read it. Barker did remember him, though the process was a lot harder in reverse, given how many people he'd met who loved his book.

"Book club murder!" Barker recalled, clicking his fingers in a flash. The young PC's face lit up. "Lynn Sweet. Died in my wife's café. Poisoned by a fellow member put up to it by Lynn's flatmate."

"That's the one. Your wife was..." He held his hands out to indicate a belly bump. "How's the baby?"

"Great. At nursery." Barker wasn't here to fill in a fan on his family life. He'd remembered their single brief interaction, so he was already halfway across the cordon. If only he could remember his name. "Terrible what's happening here."

"He was a protestor, apparently," the officer admitted in a whisper, stars still in his eyes. "DI Moyes said she's crossed him before. Heard someone say his sister was a surgeon or maybe a nurse. I'm not sure. It's Riverswick's side. I'm just here from the village to make up numbers."

"They have less crime on this side," Barker said, glancing at the allotment and then back to the young PC. He suddenly remembered his name. He'd heard DI Christie say it once. Maybe hearing another familiar name had loosened it. "Did you say DI Moyes, Jake?"

PC Jake's smile grew, and he nodded. "New DI over on this side. We're still without one at the village after they gave DI Christie the boot. We all thought she was coming to join us after the time capsule cold case at the school autumn just past, but – hey, weren't you involved in that one too?"

Barker nodded, glancing at the allotment. He noticed a flash of Detective Inspector Laura Moyes's floor-length beige coat as she slipped through the metal gate. A bulb flashed behind Barker, and she skimmed in his direction. Her eyes met something behind Barker before landing on him. She squinted her recognition, and a flicker of a smile pricked her lips. Another flash, and she ducked away into the shadow of the vans blocking the narrow path.

"Johnny?" Barker turned, surprised to see the former editor. "What are you doing here? You just moved."

"I just can't keep away. I could ask you the same question. A body's been found. Do you know anything useful for my *last* last issue of *The Peridale Post*?"

Barker did, but he was distracted by a familiar yellow Mini rounding the corner and parking by the front of the mural. Jessie wasted no time jumping out and joining them on the curved path.

"What's the craic?" she asked, looking cool with her shades and backpack. The sun lit up the pink ends of her otherwise dark hair. "I got here as fast as I could. Roadworks and protests."

"Psst. Barker Brown?"

PC Jake, whatever his surname was, pulled Barker in with a jerk of his head and a pleased-with-himself grin.

Jackpot.

"I asked one of the forensics who overheard DI Moyes name the victim. Beth only told me because we kissed at the Christmas party, and she doesn't want me to tell her—"

"The name, Jake?"

"Right." He leaned in closer. "Henry Foreman. Twenty-seven. Lives just off yonder in a house with his mum."

"I overshot the age," Barker said, almost to himself. "I've seen some shocking things in my time, but never anything more alarming than that terrible attempt to bury a body."

"I thought the same," Jake said, almost gasping. "I'd bet they were disturbed and legged it."

"About two weeks ago, I'd say."

"That's what Beth said. Eh, they said you were good. When's this second book coming out, then? Are you working on anything?"

Barker stuttered for an answer. What was the current line he'd been using in responses to the emails that had yet to stop, even though he was always sure each would be the last – it wasn't in his current plans, but he'd never say never.

"He's writing it at the moment," Jessie said confidently.

"You are?" Johnny asked.

"I am?"

"Yes." Jessie flashed her eyes at him. "Remember? You told me at Johnny's wedding."

"A possible title," he whispered, unable to ignore the expectation in Jake's eyes. "I *might* be working on something."

"When's it coming out?"

Barker chuckled. "Might. But if I—"

"Excuse me." A man with silver hair, a puffed-out chest behind a cream body warmer, and about half a foot taller than any of them stood nearby, waiting to catch their attention. The rest of the group stood behind him as though he'd been nominated, and Barker's laugh must have killed his patience. "We couldn't help but overhear you say that ... the man they found was ... Henry? Henry Foreman?"

"I'm afraid so," Jake whispered. "But you can't go around telling people until it's been—"

"We need to find Coral." One of the women

gasped, her hands at her mouth, as the others sprang to life in a dithering frenzy. "Oh, she's going to be devastated."

Their search for Coral sent everyone scuttling away from the cordon in different directions before Barker could ask why. Barker didn't know Coral's surname either, but she certainly looked old enough to have a twenty-seven-year-old son.

"Interview, Barker?" Johnny prompted, his phone already tilted towards him with the fluffy microphone attachment plugged in. "Where did you find Henry Foreman?"

"With the carrots," Barker said, glancing back at the allotment and, more so, Jake's right ear, which was pointed right at them despite having stepped back. "And not here. Let's get back to the café." He glanced at Jessie. "Someone needs to tell your mother."

"Oh, you don't think she already knows?" Jessie let out a cackle as she walked backward towards her Mini. "You've lived here for how many years, and you still don't know how this place works?"

"Good point."

Barker lingered at the cordon for a moment, searching for DI Moyes. If he could catch her eye and wave her over, she might agree to meet with him away from Johnny's roving-reporter reprisal. She was in her car, biting into a cream cake. She had to know he was there, but she didn't look up.

Maybe he didn't have such a foot in the door with her.

Although Julia would.

Or his wife's best friend Roxy would.

For now, Barker had a name, and though he'd lost the chance to get his hands dirty, he was about to delve into a new case for his new client – the current tenant of Plot Seven at Henderson Allotments

5

"Johnny, what are you doing here?"

"With the number of times I've heard that question today, I'm beginning to think people don't want me around," Johnny said as he let the café door close behind him. He accepted Julia's hug all the same. "The new editor quit on the first day, so I said I'd perform one last juggling act."

"Of course we want you around, you wally." Roxy grabbed him in a half-hug, half-headlock. "We," she said, swaying her finger between Julia and herself, "never wanted you to move in the first place. I know we only waved you off last week, but look at you, my how you've grown! I bet Leah isn't happy that you're skipping out on the first week unpacking your new house."

"It's an apartment," he corrected with a slight shrug, though Julia had seen the penthouse Leah had picked, and it was anything but modest. "And she paid someone to do all that before we even walked in. It's all sorted."

"Of course she did," Roxy said, leaning back and peering through the window. "Ah, here he is. He's got some explaining to do."

Johnny sat at the table Roxy had staked her claim to, nearest the counter, as Julia readied herself behind it. Roxy cracked her knuckles, clearly ready for battle, but Julia prepared for a conversation. Despite the theories Roxy had been spinning, Barker's explanation would no doubt be as simple as Melissa's had been.

"You already know, don't you?" Jessie asked as she bounded in, slinging her backpack down on the counter. "About the—"

"Body at the allotment?" Julia filled in the rest with a nod. "Roxy happened to be over that way."

"Nice over there, Barker," Roxy called out, scratching the side of her head as her brows wrinkled her forehead. "Isn't it?"

"Yes?" Barker shut the door as he looked around.

"I thought there'd be more people here. Word hasn't spread that fast."

"But Mum does know," Jessie said.

"The whole truth," Roxy said, darting a glance at Julia.

Julia cleared her throat gently and shook her head at Roxy. As much as she appreciated her friend backing her up, she'd already decided to veto Roxy's suggestion to pretend like she knew 'everything' so Barker would confess to his secret allotment just around the corner. That tactic might work while interviewing a suspect, or even for a teacher questioning a naughty child, but not so much in a healthy marriage.

"You have an allotment?" Julia asked.

"Got the key this morning," he said, kissing her over the counter. He smelled as if he'd spent the day standing in the fresh air of a field. "Put my name down for one in my first week here. Did I never tell you about it?"

Julia shook her head. Not that they'd been together back then. Even though they'd met when his moving van blocked the lane down to the village, it had taken them a little longer to go on their first official date at the Comfy Corner – which had been interrupted by Barker needing to chase a suspect. Julia had gone with him, and they'd barely left each other's sides since. Certainly enough that Julia knew Barker hadn't been spending swathes of time in his secret allotment 'chopping women up' or 'growing plants for hippies' – both of which an overexcited Roxy suggested after her brush with the crime scene.

"I really did think the café would be fuller, considering a murder has just happened a stone's throw away," Barker said, taking a bite of the carrot cake he'd helped himself to. "People love to gossip."

"Carrots, Barker?" Johnny muttered, fingertips already bashing at his laptop. "After your discovery?"

"True," Barker said, going in for a second bite, "but it really is delicious."

"Thank you." Julia accepted the compliment, though she was too busy taking in the café to say much else. Barker was right. A death so close should have packed the place.

"Julia?" Dot's voice bellowed from behind them as she slipped through the back door Julia had opened to let in the fresh air after Roxy had helped herself to toast – and burnt it miserably. "You'll never guess what just happened in Riverswick."

"We know," Jessie, Barker, Johnny, and Roxy chorused.

"All right." Dot skidded to a halt behind the beads before parting them with her fingers. "Keep your hair on. I'm only reporting what I just heard on the telephone. One of Percy's old magic friends has an allotment there. A great big tall fella."

"Riverswick?" Julia echoed, looking at the café once again. "That'll explain it. I thought the allotments were down near my dad's shop, where Alfie and Billy had that builder's yard?"

"And then left at the big tree and 'just around the way,'" Barker said, his fingers forming the quotation marks. "It's barely on the border."

"Won't matter," Dot announced, lingering between the beads and beckoning Julia into the kitchen with a waft of her hand. "It'll take a slower news day than this to have a *Riverswick* murder light up this place."

"Did Peridale gain an enemy while I was away?" Jessie asked, looking up from the embossed copy of *Romeo and Juliet* Barker had picked out. "When's the war?"

"Note to self," Johnny said, "don't mention Riverswick on the front page."

Julia followed her gran into the kitchen. Dot paced on the other side of the island, chewing at her thumb. Julia was taken back to the evenings she'd spent watching Dot do the same in front of the mantelpiece in her living room whenever she wanted to cook up ideas for their now-defunct watch group.

"I know it's only Riverswick—"

"Peridale's mortal enemies, apparently?" Julia

interrupted, picking up the cup of tea she'd abandoned earlier. She took a sip, and though cold, it was still as sweet and minty as she liked it.

"Well, they're being..." Dot stopped her pacing in front of the fridge and circled her hand in a loop like a barrel spinning down a hill trying to grab hold of something. She tilted her head back, and yelled, "Jessie, what did you say that thing was when normal places get all poshed up? Genderification?"

"*Gentrification*," Jessie called back, with Johnny and Barker echoing the same in stereo.

Dot wiggled her finger as though she'd known all along and started moving again. "They've got all those fancy new houses and shops, and they've even had electric charging stations installed all down the high street. And have you seen their roads, Julia? They're as smooth as butter, and we're over here tripping over centuries-old cobbles and leaping over potholes as big as Cheddar Gorge!" She paused to inhale, though the pacing sped up. "Henderson Place, Riverswick's brand-new housing development, of which your sister has recently become a resident, has been built right next to Henderson Allotments."

"What a strange coincidence."

"*Coincidence*?" Dot's voice came out in a strained croak. "It means we have a reason to go looking around! Someone will have seen something. We can get the jump on them, get on the ground, and..."

The tinkling of the bell over the door brought Julia's attention back into the café. Riverswick or not, it was a Friday, and Julia didn't have time to go racing off to snoop with her bored grandmother.

"Gran, I love you, but I'm at work," Julia said, stepping back through the beads.

Dot huffed and gave her hands one final flap before leaving out the back in a cloud of defeat. As fun as snooping around the countryside with her grandmother would be, Julia wished she'd asked on a Sunday.

"Barker?" Julia whispered over the top of the display case filled with sandwiches, as the customer, a woman Julia had never seen before, stared in bewilderment at the menu on the wall. "Did you manage to get a name?"

Jessie peeled back the blinds in the front bay window of what had been, until last week, Leah and Johnny's cottage. Julia and Barker's cottage looked tiny across the lane, though the layout was pretty much the same as the cottage she was standing in – not that they looked anything alike otherwise.

"I thought the place had sold," Jessie said, her eyes grazing past the FOR SALE sign that had been jutting from the perfectly pruned rosebushes since the end of last year.

"We're in the solicitors' phase," Johnny replied, his fingers still scrolling on his laptop, just as they'd done since he'd sat down in the bucket chair by the lamp shaped like a pineapple. "Sit down."

"I'm scared of touching anything." Jessie perched on the plump sofa and craned her neck as she looked around the ultramodern living room. "It looks like the pictures of those new apartments at Wellington Heights I'll never be able to afford."

"You and half the village," he said, glancing up. "James Jacobson's failed attempt to start a property empire in Peridale. He's already put half of them up for rent." He let out a laugh, and Jessie didn't miss the sting of the venom. "Don't suppose you've seen much of him in that house he built down the lane where Barker first lived?"

"Still hasn't taken the scaffolding down, though it looks like it's been finished for months. I've never met the guy. His son owns that bar in the village."

"I know, and he won't answer any more of my questions." Johnny's cheeks flushed as he scrunched his brows at the screen before finally smiling. "Ah, here he is. *Riverswick Gazette*'s Court Announcements.

Our recently deceased friend, Henry Foreman, has about a decade of offences, though he's never been sentenced to time inside. Most recently, he was arrested last spring for 'supergluing himself to the entrance of Henderson Place,' which ground construction work to a halt. Oh, and in June for sabotaging equipment ... and again in September for chaining himself to the door of the first show home. This guy is a big-time ecowarrior, and oh – this one is the most recent offence."

"And final."

Johnny frow ned as his nose moved closer to the screen. "And it's different. He was arrested for assaulting a doctor. Dr Adnan Khan. Henry was given a suspended sentence for GBH in the first week of January, and Dr Khan was granted a restraining order against Mr Foreman."

"That is a little different."

Jessie joined Johnny behind his chair and looked at his laptop over his shoulder. He was reading an article about the assault. Jessie couldn't see the words from where she stood, but she could see the picture. Anyone else would have gone to court in a suit, but Henry Foreman had turned up looking like he'd just clocked off from a garden centre. He wore a khaki shirt, open at the chest to show a clutter of wooden necklaces; brown cargo shorts; and flip flops. His hair, thin at the front, was pulled off his face in a low ponytail.

"Doesn't look like a guy I'd expect to have been arrested so many times," Jessie thought aloud. "Though, what does *that* look like? He must have really cared about these causes."

"Doesn't say why he attacked this doctor, but Dr Khan was quoted as saying that 'Mr Foreman has been harassing him and his wife all year.'"

"Does it say why?"

"Nope."

"What about why he was protesting?" Jessie swung back and clapped her hands together, checking out the glamourous dining room that had the same industrial feel as Happy Bean. "He clearly didn't want those houses to be built. This place is really nice, by the way."

"Isn't it?" Johnny sighed, closing the laptop. "Only got to live here for a few weeks. Leah thought redecorating for the sole purpose of selling would work, so she had the whole thing done in a week, but that's Leah. Rearranged and planned our wedding in less time." He laughed, thumbing the wedding band on his left hand. "I might give her a call and see if she's finished at the wedding fair. Longest we've been apart in a while."

"How romantic."

"And speaking of romance," Johnny said, patting Jessie's backpack on the sofa as he passed, his phone already at his ear, "we'll go over your coursework when I get back. In the meantime, why don't you keep digging on my laptop? If you find anything, don't be scared to write it up. I need as many inches for the last issue as possible."

"You want me to write for the paper?"

"Why not?"

Jessie's mouth failed to respond the first time she parted her lips, but she tried again. "Did you miss the part where I told you I got a D on my mock exam?"

"Exams are easy. You just have to say what the exam board wants you to say. Get researching. If Leah answers, I'll probably have ten minutes before she needs to rush off for something, so that's how long you have to find out what you can about Henry Foreman."

Johnny pulled the door into the frame, so Jessie picked up the laptop and carried it to the sofa. She placed it on the wooden coffee table after shimmying a bowl filled with wooden balls to the side, leaned forward, cracked her knuckles, and started typing.

"Ten minutes," she said. "And he said it like it would be a challenge."

Barker held his breath and resisted the urge to lean further into the bush as the patrol officer walked by with his torch. The beam of light illuminated the flies hovering in the lingering heat and flashed inches from Barker. He flinched deeper into the rustling thorns anyway. Clenching his eyes shut, he expected the torchlight to burn through his eyelids momentarily, but the officer's footsteps carried on.

Barker had returned home to change into the only worn-looking, neutral items of clothing he could find, though Jessie had pointed out that she thought he looked like someone playing a farmer in a play. His fellow allotment holders had been avoiding him at every opportunity too, so he hadn't been able to extract any additional information. Eavesdropping had confirmed that Henry was Coral's son. Otherwise, he'd kept up the appearance of busyness by carrying around anything that wasn't nailed down. He walked half a tree stump up and down the path at least six times, but it was enough to keep the police from paying him too much attention after they shrank the cordon back to cover only Plot Seven.

"D'you think Beth will go out with me if I ask?" PC Jake Puglisi's innocent tone rose above the other sounds. DI Moyes had called out the unusual surname enough times. "I really fancy her. She's my type. She's funny, smart, and—"

"Are you *her* type?" a woman replied, a bite in her voice. "Just leave her alone, Jake. You know she's got a boyfriend, and he's a black belt in karate."

"I can fight, and she said she'd dump him."

"While drunk at the Christmas party."

"Still," Jake said, optimistic. "She said it."

"Forget Beth. Did you lock up?"

"I'm not thick," he said before adding, "and I could easily take him. Those belts don't even mean anything."

As their voices drifted away, Barker squinted into the dark, looking for the reflective panels on their uniforms. A flash of the patrol officer's torch lit them up as they climbed the slope towards the mural.

"And just back up the way."

Barker let himself breathe normally for the first time since he'd dived into the bushes during the patrol's first lap, after they'd announced that everyone should leave their allotments for the day. That had been around sunset, and the sky above was as black as tar. More importantly, the crime scene was silent.

Barker waited for the patrolling officer to head in the opposite direction before making his move. He followed the path back to the top, turning where he'd first heard Jake's voice. He'd spent most of the day trying to blend in, and there'd been another identical path he could have used behind his row the whole time. A couple of streetlamps tried their best to light up the path, but they were blocked by a dense row of trees on either side of the path. Through the trees on the other side, he noticed a red brick wall. A new wall. The rain hadn't fully washed away the dust left by the builders, nor had the weeds had a chance to grow back against the border. He stood on tiptoes to try to peer over it, but it was at least seven feet high.

A swish of the officer's torch pushed Barker against the nearest allotment. He froze as the beam scanned from left to right. Chancing a glance, he darted forward, only to run straight back again as the torchlight danced dangerously close to his nose. His allotment was three down; the officer was seven. He hazarded another glance as the beam stretched across the red stone wall.

Plot Seven had a corrugated metal back, and there was no way in without making a racket. Plot Five, however, had only a wooden fence, and the slats had been placed in a way that suggested the keyholder wasn't as bothered about security. Barker slipped inside and instantly recognised it as Coral's patch. Her allotment looked like something from a storybook: beds flourished with tomatoes and cabbages while a scattering of wind chimes sang them lullabies. Barker had a feeling that the chimes he'd been hearing all day would be Coral's. He thought about looking around to find out more about the mother of the victim, but time was short, and there was an unattended crime scene to get to.

Using a wheelbarrow already positioned by the dividing wall, Barker pulled himself over and down into somebody else's tomatoes. A couple detached and popped under his shoe. He froze and waited for the torch to catch him, but it didn't come his way. Keeping his head down, he crossed the allotment between his and Coral's and pulled himself over the fence.

"I'm in," he couldn't resist saying to himself.

Henry had long gone, but by the looks of it, forensics had combed over the entire place. He stifled a laugh because they'd saved him a job. The beds looked fresh enough to plant seeds and bulbs ... as soon as he figured out how to do it.

First, he had to answer a question that had been bugging him since Julia first pointed it out back at the café.

"Avoid my gran," she'd said, sending him off with more carrot cake, "and figure out how they got into the allotment. You said the door was locked, so somebody must have had a key."

He rested a hand against the pocket containing his spare key. He'd have used it on the front gate if he'd had to. The Council had only given him one key, which he'd dutifully handed over to the first officer who'd arrived at the scene.

Not for the first time in his life, he was grateful for his late mother's advice regarding new keys.

"Before you put that key anywhere," she'd said, handing him his first house key when he was thirteen, "you take it down to the locksmith's and you ask to have two spares cut. You put one in a drawer and give another to someone you trust."

Would the shed have a lock? He'd at least be safe from discovery in there. His only other option was to climb over the back fence, which would make just as much noise from this side. The police would have combed over the shed, so he didn't expect they'd missed anything, but he'd come all this way. Walking between two fresh beds of soil, he smiled at the sight of the open lock missing a padlock.

"Bingo," he said to himself. "Oh my—"

Barker choked out a laugh as Detective Inspector Laura Moyes scrambled up from where she'd been sitting on a plant pot. She ripped wireless earbuds from her ears as the trails of her electronic cigarette smoke drifted up from her nose.

"What are you doing here?" he asked.

"I could ask you the same thing," she said, coughing and wafting away the smoke. "Breaking and entering a crime scene? A retired detective should know better."

"My name is on the place, as of this morning," he said, while Moyes bent down to pick up the phone that had slid from her lap when he'd startled her. She'd been watching a cooking video of someone icing an intricate-looking cake that resembled a fantasy castle. Not what he'd have expected from the stylish DI, but he certainly hadn't expected to find her sat on a plant pot waiting for him like Andy Pandy, either. "You were expecting me, weren't you?"

"The jig is up," she said into a radio she'd pulled from her belt. "Great job, guys. He got in without you finding him. Reward's off the table." She clicked the radio back to her belt and, after a deep inhale, steadied her hands on her hips. "I saw you dive into that bush hours ago. I was waiting for you to stumble out, but when you didn't, I realised we could have a little fun with you. And here I was, thinking I'd be having a quiet time in Riverswick."

"Is that why you're here? You were on cold cases last time I saw you."

"And you were a PI," she said, looking him up and down. "Now you're … an old man about to write his second book? PC Puglisi hasn't been able to shut up about it all day."

"I've heard. And I'm still a PI, which is why I'm

here. The key holder of this allotment has hired me to find out why he found a body there on his first day."

DI Moyes smiled dryly. "And how much will you be paying yourself?"

"A nice bonus, if I figure it out."

"Before I do, you mean?" DI Moyes gave her electronic cigarette a puff before slotting it away. "Well, it's your lucky day, Mr PI, because I think we can help each other on this case. Tell me what you know so far, and I might have something for you."

"So, this wasn't a surprise social visit?"

"I could still have you arrested."

Despite her tone, she was smiling, though her gaze was anything but jovial. Her stare always made Barker feel like she was playing chess with him, yet he hadn't been given the pieces.

"Who says I know anything?" he countered, opening his palms as he leaned against a shelf of plant pots. The shelf leaned with him, and he quickly moved away before the pots fell. At least he wouldn't have to buy any when he got around to gardening. "This could be my first attempt to find out information."

"I've seen you trying to grill everyone all day," she said, tilting her head at his raggedy khaki coat. "And despite your current get-up, which is a terrible attempt at a disguise, by the way, you're still a DI at heart. So, what do you know?"

Barker folded his arms, and despite the threat of an arrest, knew the ball was in his court. She wanted to know what he knew, so whatever she had to exchange must be good.

"A man in his late twenties was murdered a fortnight ago and partially buried in an allotment two doors down from his mother's. I also know he has a nurse sister who—"

"Doctor," she cut in. "Continue."

"The exact time and cause of death, I don't know. Nor do I know if he was buried on the same day he died." He paused and waited for Moyes to fill in more gaps, but her smile only lifted at the corners. *Not that easy.* "From the looks of his online presence, he's a keen environmentalist who has been protesting the building of that housing development, which, judging by that red wall over there, wasn't a success. He also assaulted a doctor, but I don't know why."

Moyes nodded, taking in what he'd said as she stepped forward. "Right then, so basically nothing I don't know already. I suppose it's your lucky day. You mentioned knowing Coral."

"I spoke to her briefly on my way here this morning."

"During her interview, she mentioned meeting you," she offered in a low voice. "Not that I could get much out of her. She doesn't trust the lot of us as far as she can throw us, but I can't say I blame her. She's been getting herself arrested several times a year at one protest or another for decades. Coral says she doesn't know anything and hasn't seen Henry in two weeks. Apparently, that wasn't strange."

Barker thought back to the woman with the catlike green eyes and bushy curls, and though he hadn't spent much time with her, he couldn't imagine she'd lie about something connected to her son. He immediately reproached himself, catching his own biases. Any short older lady with a waddle in her walk and a mission on her mind never failed to remind him of his mum, but that didn't automatically mean she was innocent.

"Maybe she doesn't know anything," he suggested. "But if she wouldn't open up to you, there's no saying she'll talk to me."

"Oh, she will." Moyes patted Barker on the shoulder as she passed him. "She referred to you as 'that handsome new man' when I spoke with her. Ask her about the ring, handsome new man."

"What ring?"

"That's why I want you to ask her," DI Moyes said, continuing talking as she left the shed. "She said something along the lines of 'I hope this isn't about that ring,' and then wouldn't elaborate when questioned about it."

"I'll see what I can do."

Alone in the dark shed, Barker stared out at the freshly turned-over beds. The soil could wait, but could Coral? PC Puglisi has mentioned she lived 'off yonder' with a general wave of his arm somewhere east. Even if Barker could find her house in the dark, he wasn't sure Coral would appreciate a visitor so late, especially after a day of losing her son and being grilled by the police about it.

"Mr Brown?" DI Moyes called, patting the door. He hadn't realised she'd been waiting with it open. "If you please, now would be a great time to vacate my crime scene."

While DI Moyes checked her watch, Barker slid one of the spare keys into a drawer in the cluttered shed. *His* cluttered shed. He took a last look around, silently promising that he'd be back to use it for its actual purpose.

6

*J*ulia woke the following morning in sweat-soaked sheets, though she'd somehow managed a fair night's sleep. She'd batted away the temptation to unpick the details surrounding Henry's murder – no easy task, considering Barker's choice of pillow talk.

"Crikey, is the heating on?" Barker grumbled, clicking his tongue against the roof of his mouth as he tossed the duvet off in one swoop. "Sorry, Mowgli," he said as nails skidded across the floorboards. "I feel like I just woke up on holiday."

Julia tugged at the edge of the curtains above the cold radiator for a blast of the brightest morning sun she'd seen all year. She could make out Olivia's morning babble in the room next door. "Time to get the day started. It's going to be a busy one."

"A body will do that."

"I doubt the body you found in Riverswick is going to factor in much today," she said, tossing Barker his dressing gown as he checked his phone like a short-sighted mole waking up at the wrong end of the day. "First scorching Saturday of the year, and Easter is around the corner. Could have done with that extra pair of hands today."

"Do you—"

"No." Julia silenced him with a smile and a kiss before passing him his glasses. The last thing she needed was a day of 'what button did you say opens the till drawer?' during the juggling act she and Jessie had nailed down, but he didn't need to know that. "Besides, it's the first day on your new case. I know your boss personally, and I will be reporting back to him."

"Must be close to you, this boss?" Barker tugged Julia's arm in, and they shared another kiss. "He sounds handsome."

"Coral's second-hand compliment has gone to your head. But yes, he is."

After a rushed breakfast, Julia left Barker and Olivia to enjoy their leisurely Saturday morning, and she threw herself into the café. Her prediction of a busy day turned out to be as accurate as any reading Evelyn had ever given. Jessie had to drive to the nearest supermarket to buy the few fans they had left in stock.

"Did you hear about that ecowarrior getting whacked in Riverswick?" Ethel White, one the village's top busybodies – second only to Dot – said somewhere after three in the afternoon. "That's what you get for ruffling so many feathers, I suppose. Shouldn't have tried so hard to stop those houses being built."

"What houses?"

"Some new development," Ethel said with a dismissive gesture in the general direction of Mulberry Lane. "Did you hear about the theme of this year's spring fete Easter hat contest? I don't know what Father David was thinking, but I do hope the weather holds up until then."

As Julia had predicted, Ethel White summed up the mood of the day. The murder of Henry Foreman would have been an all-you-can-eat buffet of spat-out suspect names and twisted theories had he been found a stone's throw over the border, but anything that happened in Riverswick, no matter how shocking, would only ever be a side dish in Peridale.

The day ended with Julia soaking her feet in a bucket of warm bubbles. She woke in a similar sweat on Sunday, though she wasn't in such a hurry to get the day started. After a lazy breakfast in the garden, serenaded by birds in the sunshine, Julia followed Barker to Henderson Allotments for her first tour. So far, the only stops had been 'here's the shed' and 'here's where I found him,' but Barker promised vegetables for all soon.

"I knew I was right," Dot cried, spreading the map she'd found in the shed on an upturned barrel. Julia glanced away from watching Percy's bulb-planting lesson to her gran's shiny fingernail tapping on a patch of forest. "Sue's house is part of that" – she jabbed her finger towards the corrugated panels at the back of the allotment and beyond – "new housing development. You know they built seventy-four of them? She swore she was still in Peridale, but I had a feeling when we walked all that way to see her house that we'd slipped out of the postcode."

Julia tilted her head and took a closer look at the map, wondering when she'd missed the start of the Riverswick hate train. Maybe the 'genderfication' had started when she'd been in the cosy cottage bubble of her maternity leave. She checked on Olivia, who was still content in the wheelbarrow in the shadow of the trees. Bruce, the French bulldog, was flat out on his back under the barrow, but Lady, the white-haired

Maltese, hadn't stopped doting on Olivia since Dot and Percy had shown up.

"This entire area used to be Henderson Vale," Dot said, circling a patch of greenery next to the detailed drawing of the allotment. "Part of the bigger Henderson Forest, which stretches out all the way to Howarth Forest in our village." She flipped over a few pages, but Julia was still having a hard time believing that she wasn't in her own village. After a brisk five-minute walk, she could be talking to her dad next to a 19th-century oak wardrobe. "You can't tell where one forest starts and the other begins, but judging by how far that wall stretches, I'd say they've chopped down half the lot. It's a travesty."

"A true tragedy, my love," Percy agreed, patting down the soil. "But it really is that simple, Barker."

"How is it you ended up with an allotment that you don't know how to use, anyway?" Dot asked, looking around the place with a wrinkled nose. "You've had years to figure out the basics."

"I thought I'd be waiting for even more years." He shrugged as he looked down at the map. "Don't suppose there's a house on there? Coral Foreman lives around here somewhere, but I can't find anything on the map on my phone."

Dot spread the map out further, shaking off the dust that had gathered in the years it had spent yellowing in a drawer in the shed. Unclasping her handbag, she pulled out a magnifying glass and a small silver pen. After a final scan, she circled four squares surrounded by trees.

"These appear to be dwellings." She folded the map, crammed it under her arm, and gave Julia an expectant throat clearing. "Why don't we go and pay Sue a visit? See how she's settling in. There's a path that'll lead us to the front of the development. Barker, you can have the map back when we're done."

"You found the map in my shed."

"Won't be long," Dot called, waving over her head as she dragged Julia towards the gate. "It'll give you time to figure out how to hold the shovel."

"I can't believe I didn't notice them before," Dot said, sounding as aghast as Julia felt. "They're so big."

"And shiny."

"Maybe it was foggy?" Narrowing her eyes even further, Dot stuck out her head and planted her hands on her hips, giving the perfect impression of a chicken. They'd been standing on the corner outside Sue's house, staring at the red brick box in the distance, for at least five minutes. "You can't see a thing through those gates, but at least we know where the other side of that red brick wall is. C'mon, let's get in. I'm baking out here, and I only have Factor 15 on. What are you on?"

"Fifty," Julia replied while her gran gave Sue's new doorbell a few stabs. She couldn't look away from the pearly gates at the end of the impossibly long road. "It looks like this entire housing development has been built on the driveway for whatever's behind that wall."

"It's the reason we're all here," Sue said, her voice pulling Julia away for the first time since they'd arrived at the lower end of Henderson Place. "A surprise mid-afternoon visit on a Sunday. To what do I owe the honour?"

"You said Peridale," Dot said as she caught her breath, barging past Sue, who had a teary-eyed and red-faced Dottie balanced on her hip. "This is Riverswick."

"Please, Gran, come on in," Sue said when Dot was already in the kitchen. The sisters shared a grin. "Quite honestly, you couldn't have come at a worse time, but now that you're here, you can stick the kettle on."

Julia gladly followed her sister into her three-storey red brick house at the end of a row of four identical houses, one row of the duplicates that ran all the way to the gates. If Julia's cottage of crumbling golden Cotswold stone were to turn up in Sue's pristine back garden behind her all-white and copper kitchen, it would look like a rotting potato ditched in a bowl of ripe green apples.

Julia quickly filled the kettle, trying to figure out what she'd walked in on. Pearl, Dottie's twin sister, was blubbering at the counter, an orange plaster stuck to her forehead. Julia saw a matching bruise underneath a pink plaster on Dottie's forehead, only on the other side.

"Get the one with the kitchen island, Neil said," Sue said, passing Julia four mugs. Was Neil upstairs? "Pearl went one way, Dottie the other, and they met at the corner like two conkers determined to knock each other's brains out, but that's three-year-olds for you." She rubbed both their cheeks with a finger each while peering down her nose at the watch pinned to her breast pocket. "Fifteen minutes." Craning her neck, she called out, "Remind me if you take sugar, Nadia. My brain has fallen out my back end."

"Just one," a woman croaked back.

"Nadia?" Julia mouthed as she passed Sue a teaspoon for the sugar.

"Friend from work. We're on our lunch break. The poor girl broke down, and I got her out of there so she could catch her breath. She was already exhausted. Nobody takes as many shifts as Nadia, and she's the last person who needs the money." The final part came out the quietest. "Someone she went to school with was murdered."

So close to the allotment, could it be a coincidence?

"Wouldn't be Henry Foreman, would it?" Julia asked. "I did text you about Barker finding that body at the allotment, but I didn't hear back."

"I've been busy." Sue cast her hands at the cardboard boxes stacked in the dining room that hadn't moved since the last – and only – time Julia had been to the house. Next to them, Dot was taking in the art on the wall over the sideboard, her hands folded behind her back. "So that's why you're here, is it?" Sue said. "Back to your snooping. You two have too much time on your hands."

The venom in her sister's voice shocked her, and Julia didn't miss the way Sue had been evading her attempts at eye contact since they'd turned up unannounced.

"Less of that tone." Dot turned, shock scrunching her wrinkles. "We obviously care about you, Sue."

"Obviously," Julia whispered, rubbing her sister's shoulder. Sue tensed, so Julia pulled back. "How are you?"

"I'm fine." It came out with a sigh. "I could go into detail about the mismanagement of the ward or our pay, but what difference would it make? I'm just trying to get on with things."

"You're acting like you don't have a choice, dear," Dot said, softening to Sue's level. "It's Sunday. You should be relaxing."

Sue didn't hold back her laughter, and the venom lacing it was just as shocking on a second hearing. Julia had never heard anything like it from her sister. "Some of our worlds don't work like—"

A gentle throat clearing cut Sue off, and she spun to the double glass doors leading to the living room and its mid-century-modern décor. It looked as much like a magazine spread as Leah's old cottage, but here, the photographers had left and the toddlers taken over. A woman in a blue nurse uniform that matched Sue's stepped into the room. A caramel-coloured headscarf was wrapped around her hair and secured at her left temple with a gold pin.

"Nadia?" Sue prompted when the woman didn't talk.

"I think I might go home and clean up," she said, eyes firmly on the chevron floorboards. "My eyeliner looks a proper state, and we've got another six hours on shift."

"Nadia, nobody will blame you if you—"

"I'm not leaving you in the lurch," she said,

smiling shakily as she backed out of the room. "I won't be long."

Sue checked her watch and took a deep gulp of her coffee, swiping her keys off the counter before letting each twin down to the floor. "I'll drive you. We'll never get back in time if you walk there and back. You two can show yourselves out. Door locks behind you."

"Wait, before you go." Dot spun around, hooking a thumb at the large canvas covered in pale yellow and blue brushstrokes. "I have to ask. What is it supposed to be?"

"I dunno," Sue said. "It was here when we moved in. The place was practically fully furnished."

"And you still haven't got around to unpacking," Dot said. "All of this happened rather quickly. I thought you couldn't get a mortgage? And how did you sell your house so fast? I was talking to Johnny this morning, and it's taken them months."

"An offer came up that we couldn't refuse," Sue said. For a second, Julia thought Sue was going to stop and explain, but she looked to the twins already toddling down the hallway to Nadia, waiting by the door. "Look, I'll tell you about it another time. Thanks for dropping by. I'd apologise for how you caught me, but, well, this is it these days."

Sue tossed her hands out and let them clap to her

side before hurrying down the corridor like she was in the hospital ward and someone had called a code.

"We need to do something," Julia said the moment the door shut behind her. "You're right. She isn't fine."

"And despite her claims, she's not even trying to hide it anymore," Dot said, chewing at her lip as she looked around the house. "Sue's problem is that she won't come willingly. We're a family of independent women, and that can get in the way. And what do you think she meant by 'made her choice'? You don't think she's joined some sort of nurses' cult, do you?"

"You've got cults and sacrifices on the brain."

"Percy and I watched one documentary about a cult on our tablet, and the next thing you know, the algorithm" – pronounced *algae-rhythm* – "is suggesting them nonstop. They are rather fascinating. All it takes is a charismatic leader with an idea, and boom, next thing you know, forty people are dead."

"We only have one dead person so far."

"Someone has to be the first, dear," Dot grumbled, as though she knew something nobody else did. "You watch. There'll be a body in every allotment soon enough."

"I don't think she's joined a cult," Julia said, sipping the hot tea she'd only just made for herself. Her eyes followed the movement at the kitchen window as Sue's car drove up the road towards the gates. "What do we do, Gran?"

Dot looked around. "For once, I don't know, love, but we can start here."

A clap of her hands made Julia spill some tea into the sink, but she couldn't pull herself away from the window. She'd assumed Sue would come back down after turning her car around, but she was driving right up to the gates.

What had Sue said about whatever lay beyond the gated box when she'd opened the front door?

It's the reason we're all here.

"We'll just nip in when the gates open and have a little look around," Dot said with a firm nod, shifting her weight from one foot to the other. "We're up to nothing illegal."

So why does it feel like we are?

Julia hadn't needed convincing to follow up her gran up the freshly paved road to the gates after their whiparound of Sue and Neil's downstairs. She glanced up at the security camera domes on either side of the gate, wishing they'd gone straight back to the allotments.

"If we were doing something wrong, they'd have

come out by now," Dot whispered into Julia's ear, as though reading her mind. "Two nurses go behind a secret gate that has no sign and a wall too high for either of us to climb … smells a little fishy, don't you think? Speaking of which, how many eyes does this girl have to line? Do you think there's another road out of Riverswick's very own Area 51? Oh! Did you hear that an alien killed a woman's husband and made it look like a stroke?"

"Where'd you hear that?"

"Jessie."

"Then I think Jessie is pulling your leg." Julia couldn't help but laugh, though she made a mental note to congratulate Jessie on convincing her gran that aliens were visiting Peridale. "Something Sue said made it sound like Nadia didn't need to work, so my guess is more houses. Let's just go back to the—"

Dot held her finger up. "Shh! My ears never fail. Those gates are about to open. Up against the wall. Do you think they'll swing in or out? Get back, Julia!"

The gates swung neither in nor out, but upwards. Panels Julia hadn't previously noticed in the otherwise smooth metal gates concatenated like a paper fan closing in on itself. The two fans sank into the walls, and Sue's white car crawled out, just as Dot's fingers crawled around Julia's shoulder to drag her behind the angular bushes lining the road.

"We won't have long," Dot said, patting Julia. "Let's go."

Dot scurried away as Julia watched Sue and Nadia drive off. They were both in the car, and nothing seemed amiss, yet something didn't feel right.

"Oh, Julia, you're going to have to meet me back there."

Julia turned and ducked to see the last of her gran's face as the gates slid back down, trapping them on either side.

"I did tell you we wouldn't have long, dear. I'll have a poke around, and I'll meet you back there. I'll figure something out."

"Gran..."

"I'll be fine," she called, her voice already shrinking away. "If you never see me again, tell Percy I love him and to watch out for flying saucers."

Reluctantly leaving her gran on the other side of the wall, Julia headed back to the allotment with Nadia on her mind. Sue's nurse friend – and Henry Foreman's school friend – had been right there, barely hiding her distress. If Julia was right about what was beyond the gates, Nadia lived within the very walls Henry had spent his final year alive protesting.

The same walls beside which he'd been found murdered.

Coincidence or not, Julia needed to speak to Nadia.

A security guard frogmarched a dazed Dot back to the allotment, who stopped babbling requests for directions to the nearest post office as soon as the guard released her with a warning.

"I saw the tops of some glass buildings before they grabbed me, but not much else. If only I'd had my camera. I'm telling you, Julia, something strange is going on in that place. You heard Sue. An offer came up that she couldn't refuse. Mark my words. That girl *has* joined a cult!"

Julia didn't want to speculate until she'd spoken to Sue again. Hopefully, when she wasn't so rushed off her feet and had more than a few minutes to talk. Of course, the fact that her sister never seemed to have this time was part of the problem.

Once Percy convinced Dot that they should get the dogs back for their dinner, Julia and Barker relocated their lazy Sunday to the cottage. After having Jessie around for a roast dinner – not that she looked up from her tablet much – Julia tucked Olivia in and fell into bed with a full belly and a full mind, ready to set off running in the morning.

"It should be Melissa's first day tomorrow," Julia said behind a yawn, as Barker settled into the pillow next to her. "Either way, I'm in. Something strange is happening here."

"I knew it wouldn't take long." He mirrored her yawn. "Tomorrow, I'm going to find Coral's house. And I need to discover who built Henderson Place, because they're my prime suspect right now."

Long after Barker fell asleep, Julia was still awake, not worrying about her café's new starter or the case but about her sister. No matter how long she spent spinning in the sheets, disturbing Mowgli at the foot of the bed, Julia couldn't think of how best to support Sue without needing to shake her to her senses.

Even if Sue had her walls built higher than the mysterious brick barrier at Henderson Place, there had to be a way over them.

7

Hot air hit Jessie as she walked into the wall of beeps and buzzes that was the foyer of the accident and emergency department. She'd deluded herself during her walk across the sizzling car park that she'd be greeted with freshly conditioned air like the last hospital she'd been to, but as Dot kept reminding her, she 'wasn't on the continent' anymore. A few fans lazily blew around air thick with disinfectant, but Jessie had already broken a sweat. They might not have air conditioning here like the hospitals in Spain, but the weather was performing a good impression of a Spanish afternoon.

Unlike the day she'd stepped on a rusty nail on the Spanish beach, Jessie had no reason to visit the hospital other than following a lead. As she walked past the reception desk quickly enough to give the impression that she knew where she was going, she wondered if she should have checked how legal it was to set off wandering the halls of a hospital looking for a nurse to ask her about a dead guy she had gone to school with.

Oh well, she was here now. And even without air conditioning, she was glad winter was over. While travelling, her brother, Alfie, had dubbed her the 'summer child' because of how much the weather seemed to affect her mood. *Act like you belong*, she said to herself. Advice Alfie had repeated often. He'd also been right about the hospital visit after the nail on the beach; she'd needed a tetanus jab.

"Jessie, is that you?"

Maybe she did belong.

She pushed forward a relieved smile, and her red Converse squeaked on the rubber flooring as she doubled back to the sound of Sue's voice. She'd hoped to slip in and out, undetected by her auntie, but she'd planned for the possibility of running into her. Hiding behind her sunglasses, Jessie checked out Sue, who was leaning against a reception desk with a clipboard. She and two other nurses were crowded around a box of Milk Tray. Based on Julia's description of how Sue had been the day before, she seemed in better spirits, but the hospital did seem quiet, despite the constant hum.

"I've been looking everywhere for you," Jessie said, feigning catching her breath and matching Sue's relaxed smile. "What's the occasion?"

"Jenny's got an admirer," Sue said, nodding at a woman sitting behind the reception desk who winced. Jenny's nose and cheeks glowed like glazed cherries under the always florescent light. "Karen thinks he needs to try harder than a Milk Tray if he wants to take her out. What do you think, Jessie? You can break the tie."

I'm in.

Jessie pushed her shades up into her waved hair and said, "I'd say you can't buy love with chocolate – or anything else, for that matter."

"That's what I thought," Jenny said, pushing the box forward. Jessie plucked out a chocolate shaped like a little beehive and popped it into her mouth. Rich honeycomb fizzled on her tongue after the first bite.

"Bully to that!" Karen, the third woman, said with a shake of her head. "If Paul the porter gave *me* a box of chocolates expecting to go on a date, he'd have to try a little harder."

"Caviar and Champagne?" Sue laughed.

"And don't you forget it!" Karen tugged the

clipboard from Sue and set off towards the ward. "Now, get back to work, you lazy layabouts. Can't be standing around eating chocolate all day. We have lives to save."

Sue chose the chocolate that looked like an orange segment and whispered to Jenny, "Karen ate most of the first tray, and you know she's only jealous that Paul asked you out and not her. I think you should go for it. He seems sweet."

"Should I?" Jenny asked, surprisingly looking to Jessie. Maybe she'd given the impression that she knew what she was talking about when it came to relationships. Her fingers tightened around her bag's straps; her English coursework had proven otherwise. "What do you think?"

Not knowing Paul or Jenny, Jessie said, "You should probably check he's not a serial killer first?"

Jenny snapped the lid on the chocolates and wheeled her chair back to her computer, only glancing at Jessie to see if she was still there.

Tough crowd.

Sue set off down the corridor like she knew where the fire was and planned to put it out. Jessie hurried to keep up, and Sue cast a look backwards as though she'd expected her to. "So, you were looking for me?"

"Oh, I was just in the area and wanted to see how you were."

"In the area? It's a hospital, Jessie, not Mulberry Lane." Sue shot a sharp sideways glance at her. "You're not here to talk to Nadia Khan about Henry? Gran's already called twice to grill me about what's on the other side of that wall!" She sighed. "At least I could apologise to her for how rotten I was yesterday. We'd just come off an awful trauma response after a car crash in Cheltenham city centre, we were both shattered, Nadia was upset, and I had the kids, and—"

"You really don't have to explain," Jessie said. "I hate it when Dot turns up at my house unannounced, too. There's nothing wrong with a warning text."

"Right?" Sue laughed and let out a relieved breath. "I'm glad somebody gets it. How'd you get so clever, eh? All that travelling did you the world of good."

"Just a long holiday, really."

"Own it," Sue said, looking Jessie directly in the eye. "So, you're sure you're just here to check on me and not talk to Nadia? Because if you *were* here to talk to her, she's down there to the left, and I've been bursting to go from about ten seconds after you turned up. But it's good to see you." Sue set off with a sudden waddle to her walk. "And tell your mum I'll go and see her. I owe her an apology, too."

"You probably don't," Jessie called back through cupped hands. "Hope you make it."

Sue gave her a thumbs up as she continued down

the corridor, her waddle turning to a stoop that even Dot didn't have.

Jessie appreciated the instructions, though. She walked down the corridor briskly enough to pick up a breeze, though the hospital seemed to be cooling the deeper she ventured – or perhaps she was the slowly boiling frog who'd stopped noticing.

"Which one did you say, Catrina?"

"That one at the end," a nurse with a clipboard replied as she blew on her tea, leaning against another desk. "And don't let Karen catch you up to no good in there, Nadia. You know how jealous that spinster gets."

Nadia offered a gentle laugh that Jessie could tell was for the benefit of being polite. Catrina seemed oblivious as she smiled dotingly and watched Nadia hurry down the corridor. Nadia had her head down, though she looked up at Jessie and offered a small smile long enough for Jessie to see flecks of honey in her eyes. They matched the caramel-coloured headscarf she wore – or maybe it was the other way around.

Not wanting to look like she was following the woman, Jessie waited until Nadia was on the other side of the blue curtain wrapped around the end cubicle and took another piece of Alfie's advice.

"If you ever find yourself somewhere you

shouldn't, try to blend in while you figure out your next move."

Nothing said 'blending in' in a hospital more than sitting around waiting, and Jessie didn't have to wait long. Raised voices floated towards her.

"I don't want to hear it, Nadia," a man said in a low growl. "You completely embarrassed me at dinner last night."

"I was just tired. You know Henry—"

"I don't want to hear his name!" Whomever this man was, he'd mastered sounding threatening at a low volume. "After everything that toerag put us through, whoever killed him did us a favour."

Jessie's ears pricked up, and she leaned forward on her knees to get closer as silence fell behind the curtain. She slowly lowered her backpack to the floor and unzipped it as quietly as possible.

"And don't do one thing for too long," Alfie had added as he'd plucked Champagne from the trays. The waiter had nodded at him, and Jessie and Alfie had nodded back, despite having snuck in behind the same guy out of uniform before his shift. They hadn't been invited, but it had been one hell of a party.

"Don't say that," Nadia said finally.

"I made myself clear," he said, in a calmer, though no less firm, tone. "And you knew what you were doing last night – that man dying had nothing to do with it. You told them I'd only just qualified on purpose."

"I said it because I was proud of—"

"You made me look like a total fool in front of twenty top surgeons. People I respect. Don't you know how that makes me look?"

"Nobody took it like—"

There was a beep, and Jessie wondered what in her bag had made such a high-pitched noise.

"You don't know that. I'm needed in theatre. I'll see you at home."

"I might be working double."

"Again?"

The man huffed and ripped back the curtain. Jessie's head was already down in her bag, and she kept it there, glancing each way as they walked off quickly in different directions.

"Hey, Matt," she heard Catrina say, "you'll never guess what I just saw. Dr Khan and Nadia were in there just now, probably having a cheeky snog."

If only that had been what Jessie overheard. She felt sick to her stomach. *I should have made the connection.* Sue had said Nadia's surname.

Nadia Khan.

Wife of Dr Adnan Khan.

The man Nadia's old high school friend assaulted

on New Year's Eve, just months before he wound up murdered.

Jessie considered following Nadia, but she'd opened a can of worms she hadn't been expecting and didn't know what to do with them. Though Johnny hadn't asked her, she'd wanted to keep digging to help pad the profile he was writing about Henry Foreman with some personal details.

The court records made him sound like an anonymous criminal, and his social media presence carried a strong justice message with no personality outside his bad spelling. His profile picture was a computerised mock-up of Henderson Place with a giant red cross stamped in the middle. She wasn't sure if she should pass anything she'd just heard onto Johnny, but she couldn't keep it to herself. Voices like Dr Khan's had brought prickles to her skin many times, usually because they made her feel unsafe.

Jessie knew one thing for certain, though.

Henry and Nadia must have been close to leave Nadia so upset, especially since Henry assaulted her husband on New Year's Eve. Jessie hadn't been far off whacking him herself, but that wouldn't have been very 'blending in' of her. She wanted to hope she'd caught him on a bad day, but she'd dealt with more than her fair share of men like Adnan Khan as her foster 'fathers' over the years.

Back in her car with the cold air blowing, Jessie did something she'd never have done not so long ago. With half an hour left on the parking she'd paid for, she pulled out *Romeo and Juliet*. She needed to decompress. Leaning the book against her steering wheel, she continued where she'd left off:

Yea, noise? then I'll be brief. O happy dagger!
Snatching ROMEO's dagger
This is thy sheath;
Stabs herself
there rust, and let me die.
Falls on ROMEO's body, and dies.

"Ouch!" Barker exclaimed, ripping his hand away from the gate. A rusty pin stuck out of the gate in the spot he'd grabbed – in the spot anyone would grab if they weren't looking. Remembering what Jessie had told him about the tetanus nail, he resisted cramming the pooling blood in his mouth. "That has to be on purpose, so this must be the place."

After wrestling the map back from Dot, Barker was on his second of the circled dwellings when he heard windchimes, saw wildflowers, and felt certain he'd found the right place. The boobytrap somehow confirmed that the tiny cottage with the sagging roof and smoking chimney buried in the forest belonged to Coral.

"Oi!" A clenched fist rattled a windowpane behind a bed of poppies. "Get away from my garden. This is private property."

"It's Barker, Mrs Foreman," he said, holding up a plastic shopping bag. "I wasn't sure if you'd been able to get out, so I brought you some shopping."

The curtain dropped, and Coral appeared at the latched front door emblazoned with a large NO VISITORS sign. She scanned the garden while Barker ventured up the path, suspicious of bear traps or flying poison darts after his encounter with the gate.

"You here alone?" she asked, peering at him through the gap with one giant green eye. "How'd you find me, anyway?"

"With a map."

"Impossible. My Henry had us taken off the maps." Her voice wavered on her son's name, but she carried on. "I don't know how, but he was good at stuff like that."

"Analogue saves the day." He patted the map under his arm, smearing tiny drops of blood on the paper. "Can I use your sink? I've just caught myself on a nail."

"Let's have a look."

Barker held up his finger, which permitted him access to the cottage. Coral dragged him past a sofa covered in a crocheted blanket and a giant shaggy dog too sleepy to do more than glance at Barker. She planted him at a table in a kitchen cobbled together from the same scrap that composed the allotments and produced a rusty metal tin of Quality Street. It still had the white and purple design Barker hadn't seen in decades. The new containers had shrunk to almost a quarter of the size, too. His mum had always bought him and his brothers a box every Christmas.

"Don't be a baby!" Coral barked, yanking Barker's hand closer and dabbing it with an alcohol-soaked rag with the same force he'd used to lift a coffee stain out of his office rug. "I know you Peridale folk are soft, but it's only a small cut. You'll live."

"Soft?" he said, pulling his finger away once she'd wrapped a plaster around it. His mum would have done the exact same thing with the same force. "And as for 'Peridale folk,' I'm practically a newbie."

"You from off yonder?"

Must be a catch-all unit of measurement.

"Hull, then London, then Peridale."

"Never left the county, myself." Coral dragged the shopping bag across the table, knocking off a box. A foil tray of medication fell onto the stone tiles; she scooped it up and pushed it deep into her cardigan. "Generations of my family have lived in this cottage. Used to be more of them, mind, but they keep knocking 'em down, shrinking the forest. Won't be surprised if I wake up one morning with a racetrack in front of my door. Though if I ever caught wind that they were building near me – over my dead body! For all the good protesting has done us, mind." She pushed the bag away. "I appreciate the gesture, but I won't eat any of that. Sticks to whole foods I grow myself, and I don't owns a microwave."

The cottage held few traces of modern technology. No television, either. A wind-up rotary phone balanced atop a stack of sagging volumes of the Yellow Pages directories, from back when they were still as thick a doorstop. He wasn't even sure if the Yellow Pages were still in print.

"Didn't mean to offend you."

Barker pushed forward a smile. He hadn't realised he'd gone quiet. "You didn't. I'm sure I'll figure out what to do with it."

"There's a food bank in that charity shop on Mulberry Lane. We always grow extra, and Henry takes them up." Her voice wavered again. This time, her face lost all tension as she looked at Barker, and she aged a decade as all the life vanished from her eyes. "You know what I realised today? I'll be the last one here. I thought there'd be someone of my bloodline in this forest until the ends of time, but Sharon will never take over the place."

Coral said the name like a swearword.

"Sharon?"

"My daughter." Another harsh delivery. "Lives on the other side of that gate. Number One, Henderson Place, and she'll let you know it, too."

Barker was surprised to hear about the mother and daughter's starkly different living conditions. Dot had tried her best to convince them that the flash of glass she'd seen before being escorted away was a secret medical facility or the hiding place of Mrs Hardy's aliens. It had taken Barker less than thirty seconds online to confirm that there were six detached houses, each designed in collaboration with top architects and interior designers Barker had never heard of.

They'd each sold for over a million and put to shame the houses he'd seen whenever he'd joined Julia during her maternity-leave *Grand Designs* binge-watching.

"Your daughter must do well for herself?"

"She's a surgeon," Coral said. Another word that emerged like it hurt to say. "She didn't buy that house, mind. Oh, no. Not my daughter. She wanted it all and went after it, but she quickly realised she wanted more than what reaching the top of medicine would get her, so she had to go and marry Phil Henderson. Total ferret of a man. Just saying his name makes me want to rip that place down brick by bloody brick!" Coral's fist beat down on the table, and the microwave meals in the bag jumped. "He lives at Number Six. You'd think living next door to your ex would be difficult, but those houses are so spaced out that they might as well be in different counties. Do you know what used to be there?"

"A place called Henderson Vale?"

"A place that was alive!" Another beat of her fist. "Trees, a stream, flies, spiders, fish, finches, and flowers. We'd even get wild deer when the weather was nice. It was exactly as nature intended and should never have been touched. We thought we could stop it, but it's the Council, ain't it? They're a bunch of corrupt, good-for-nothing monsters. They see perfection and slap a cubic mile of concrete on it." Coral shook her head, curls bobbing. "And I know people need somewhere to live, mind you, but you could have built an entire community where those six houses are. They could have built around what was already there and extended the community in a way that made sense for us all, but oh no. My 'son-in-law' Phil Henderson always gets his way. He's rotten to the core, I tells you. It's what being all pally with that good-for-nothing Greg Morgan gets you."

A name Barker did know.

Greg Morgan was their local MP, and Barker had briefly looked into him during the mess with the Council trying to sell off the public library to James Jacobson, a property tycoon who was slowly collecting properties across Peridale like stamps, could turn it into a restaurant.

Barker had suspected something dodgy was going on back then, given how quickly things moved, despite the protests of the village. Dot had been the most vocal, but in the end, it had taken James having a change of heart for things to stop. If it hadn't been for Barker and Julia helping him get off a murder charge after his wife was shot at a garden party, Greg Morgan would have happily watched the library go. Barker made a mental note to look into him later before letting himself get too side-tracked.

DI Moyes had sent him to Coral for a reason.

"I'm really sorry about what happened to your son," Barker said. "I know I didn't know him, but I was the one who found him."

"That woman said." She thanked him with a tight smile. "A real gem of a lad. Salt of the Earth. Would lie down on a train track for what he believed in. He was such a caring soul. Everyone who met him loved him. I don't know where I went wrong with his sister."

Coral produced a handkerchief from her cardigan sleeve and blew her nose like a trumpet. Throughout his career, Barker had heard similar sentiments from the loved ones of the recently dead, but if he was going to find out anything unusual, he needed to know the stuff Coral *wouldn't* want to talk about – all the things her son might have done that could have led to someone wanting him dead.

"Is it a coincidence that Phil's surname is—"

"Henderson?" Snarling, she shook her head. "No. That name used to mean something around here. It stood for integrity, for nature. I don't know how many generations back it was, but a man called Thomas Henderson bought this land. He saw where things were going, with industry and whatnot, and he knew how important it was to respect nature. To live alongside it, not against it. He bought this chunk of land to protect it from that greedy good-for-nothing Duncan Howarth, whose bit is in *your* village."

"I know it well," Barker said. "Runs right up to the back of the church near my wife's café. There's a house in there—"

"Howarth House," she confirmed. "As the story goes, Thomas built that place to live there with his true love, but she died. He went mad and lived alone in that forest until the day he died. That's never happened to me, mind. I don't know how the rest of you do it out there." She jerked her head 'off yonder.' "If Thomas Henderson hadn't stood in the way, your precious little village would have been forever in the shadow of the biggest wool empire in the country. Of course, consumption got him in 1852, and the plan never went ahead, but Thomas was dead by then, too. His son, Peter Henderson, named the land he inherited from his father after him and promised to respect his wishes to preserve it. Henderson Vale and the allotments came later. The vale was supposed to be a protected wildlife area, but what does that matter to the Council? I keep hearing the world is ending out there?"

"People were probably saying that in the days of Thomas Henderson and Duncan Howarth, too." Barker attempted a laugh to lighten the mood, but Coral didn't join in. She'd spoken of the two men who'd been dead a century before her birth like she'd known them personally, so he supposed her daughter was married to a direct descendant. "So, until Phil, this place was protected?"

"Henderson in name, the Devil in nature. And my daughter married him, which makes her as bad as him in my books." Coral folded her arms and nodded. "Anyway, if you only came to give me this, I think I'll be off to the allotment. I haven't seen my friends in a few days, and I'll have to face them eventually."

Barker considered leaving without bringing up the question that DI Moyes had told him to ask. He couldn't enquire about the ring Coral had mentioned in her interview – and then clammed up about – without giving away that he was working alongside the police. But Coral had been cooperative so far, and she'd given him a plaster for the cut he was certain she'd intentionally caused.

She'd handed him two new suspects, too.

Phil Henderson.

Sharon Foreman … or was it still Henderson?

Knowing where she lived, he could find out for himself. For now, he was running out of time to find out something from Coral that would please DI Moyes enough for her to keep feeding him on the case. It had always been so much easier on the other side.

"There was something else," Barker said with a confessing sigh. "I'm a private investigator. I know it's none of my business, but I'm looking into the death of your son."

"Why?"

"I found him in my allotment," he said, shrugging. "I want to bring peace to this. For him and for you. I can't promise I'll succeed, but I'm doing my best to see the bigger picture."

Coral's lips turned up into a smile for the first time since they'd met. "Have you found anything?"

"It's early days." He inhaled, but he couldn't avoid it. "A source of mine suggested that I ask you about a ring?"

Coral's eyes flashed down, and her hands shot into her cardigan pockets, rattling the box of tablets she'd scooped up from the tiles.

"I don't wear jewellery. Now, if you wouldn't mind."

"Are you sure you don't know anything about a—"

"Thank you for the shopping, Barker."

In the same way she'd dragged him in, Coral flung him out, and the chain rattled back into place. Barker wasn't sure if what he'd discovered would be enough to leech more information from the police's official investigation, but it had been enough to set off his alarm bells.

Coral Foreman was terrible at hiding her true – albeit starkly opposite – feelings towards her children, and she'd been unable to hide how much she didn't want to talk about whatever the 'ring incident' was.

And it only made Barker want to keep digging.

8

Melissa didn't turn up on Monday, so Julia wasn't surprised to find herself alone in the café at opening after a morning of baking. She'd been jotting down her thoughts on everything Barker had found out at Coral's and had drawn the same conclusion as her husband. Phil Henderson was the likeliest person to have wanted Henry out of the way for all the trouble he had caused in the lead-up to the Vale becoming the Place. A late-night text message from DI Moyes, received right after they'd finished brushing their teeth, confirmed the time and date of Henry's death: *Sometime in the early hours on the 16th. Nothing significant about that date ... other than those early hours being directly after the day*

Henderson Place launched and its first tenants moved in. Big party. Something to think about ... drink soon?

Julia was surprised Roxy hadn't told her about Laura moving so close. She'd been, in Roxy's words, 'dating a woman who travels around the country popping up white tents like a circus that juggles with old bones,' but had made no mention of the transfer. Roxy had seemed content with their steady relationship when they'd talked about it after trying to convince her that Barker chopped people up in his secret-lair allotment.

The café's first customer of the day, her gran – naturally – had already left by the time Melissa's text message, like on Friday, pinged into Julia's phone at exactly ten past the hour: *Sorry, sick.*

Julia's fingers hesitated over the tiny grey letters on the screen. *Are two strikes enough?* Melissa was still on her three-week, pre-contract trial, and as Dot had pointed out with a hammering of her finger on the counter, Julia shouldn't 'show her mercy' so early.

Okay. Hope to see you on Wednesday.

Three strikes.

There was a chance Melissa was actually sick, though Julia wasn't quite buying it. She really did hope her new starter would show up on Wednesday with a smile and a solid explanation. For now, Julia would spend Monday alone in peace and quiet, at least if her first two hours were anything to judge by. Time crawled; she'd only scheduled Melissa to show her how to check the stock levels.

Untying her apron an hour before noon, Julia pushed through the beads. So far, she'd only seen Shilpa, Evelyn, and a tourist looking for a war memorial that Julia had never heard of, which turned out to be in Riverswick.

After the text from Moyes, she and Barker had agreed to split the former couple between them. Barker would find Phil, and Julia would find Sharon, since the latter was already connected with Sue. Julia only wished she knew how to bring up Sharon without making it seem like that was all she wanted. Thoughts of Sharon weren't what had kept Julia awake for the second night in a row. The bell jangled the moment Julia draped her apron over the hook. She almost called out that they were closed but popped her head back around to see who it was first.

"Trying to save on the bills?" Sue asked, taking trepidatious steps down the middle aisle of the gloomy café. Julia missed the sunshine already, but seeing her sister on an evener keel brought some relief.

"My newbie didn't turn up, and I was just about to close. I planned to come and see you, actually." Julia fetched her jacket. Remembering Jessie's words from the night before, she added, "I *was* going to text first. Fancy getting out of here? Peridale doesn't need me today, and I could murder a Peridale pie from the Comfy Corner."

"You're talking about pies?" Sue gaped at her. "You're not mad at me?"

"Don't be silly, Sue. A bad day is a bad day, and we all have them. How are you right now?"

Sue's brow twitched in confusion, and Julia sensed that her sister was abandoning whatever script she'd prepared in advance. "I ... okay, I think. I've taken a little time off."

Julia let the relief wash over her. That was a good start. "Oh, Sue. Good for you. What are you going to do with it?"

Sue shrugged, her hands going to the strap of her handbag around her shoulder. By her expression, she wasn't partaking in whatever relief Julia was feeling.

"I could help out here?" Sue offered, bumping a chair with her hip. "If your newbie isn't going to show her face, and Jessie is going to pass her classes, you'll need an extra pair of hands." Sue paused. "She came to see me yesterday."

"I didn't send her."

Sue laughed, and Julia relaxed properly. "I know. She's a good kid, with a good head on her shoulders, but she needs to focus right now." Sue ran a fingertip across a table. "So, what do you say? I was your Saturday girl once."

"My first employee," Julia corrected. "As flattering as your offer is, *you* need to rest, and it starts right now. And yes, you can consider that an order from your big sister." Julia linked her arm through Sue's, and they set off to the door. "How long have you got?"

Sue hesitated. "It's sort of open-ended."

"Well, all the more time to spend relaxing at home with the girls – at least when they're not sprinting around the island playing conkers with their brains. But for now, Peridale pies on me, though I imagine they won't taste the same. They never really do."

"Another time?" Sue pulled her arm away and checked her watch, backing to the door. *Pie for one, it seems.* "I have somewhere to be. I came to apologise, which I thought would take longer. We'll be early if we set off now."

"Set off where?"

"You'll see."

Julia arched a brow at her cryptic sister as she set the alarm and locked the café door, but Sue's gaze was set towards the church. Julia knew *that* look in *that* direction. Past the oak tree, through the stained glass, was their mother's headstone. She joined Sue in looking towards the edge of Howarth Forest, darkened now to nothing more than a shadow by the morning gloom. She rested a hand on her sister's shoulder, and unlike last time, Sue didn't flinch away. Julia gave it a squeeze, and Sue's fingers reached up to rest on hers.

"How often do you go?" Julia asked.

"Not enough." Sue sniffed back whatever emotions had been brewing, and after a glance at Julia's vintage Ford Anglia poking out of the alley, pulled out her car keys. "Let's go. We'll take my car."

"It's abduction if you don't tell me where we're going."

"As I said, you'll see." Sue's distant stare snapped onto Julia over the top of the car as she walked around to the driver's side. Behind her and across the green, the upstairs curtains were twitching at their gran's. Julia waved, and they danced back into place. Sue turned to look, but she didn't return to Julia with the same *can you believe her?* smile Julia had expected.

Instead, her thousand-yard stare trained through Julia. "You'll see what I've been up to these past few months, and everything might start to make sense."

Explore how Shakespeare presents Juliet as a character who is determined in, blah, blah, blah.

Jessie stopped reading over the question that wasn't a question. It had stopped making sense a few rereads ago. Yawning, she wished she'd checked the time so she could know exactly how much sleep she hadn't got thanks to slithering into bed at the beginning of sunrise. She'd spent many nights in her life watching the sunrise, from sleeping on the streets to travelling with Alfie, but never for educational purposes. From Johnny's blank expression as he flipped to the second page in the stylish kitchen of the soon-to-be-sold house, she wasn't sure she'd made any progress whatsoever on her second go.

Veronica Hilt laughed out loud, and Johnny's index finger dug at his dark curls. Whether or not he realised it, his muttering lips let out sighs every few lines.

"The font is *very* big," he said, turning to the final page. "But I think this might be better. You've understood that Juliet is virtually a prisoner in her own sheltered and privileged life, with only a nurse for a friend. You didn't even touch on that in the first version."

"That's because *you* told me about it." Jessie leaned against the marble island, which left her as cold as the rest of the house was starting to; it was as much like a TV set as the interior of Happy Bean. "I'd never have got there on my own."

"But you demonstrated that you *understood* what I taught you in *your* words."

"So, that's all this is? You learn the answers and ... write them down?"

Johnny laughed and carefully placed the paper on the black marble. "People have been analysing Shakespeare to death for centuries, so what do you *think* that means?"

"That we should probably get over it and move on?"

"It means," he continued, his tightening lips letting her know it wasn't the time to use jokes to wriggle out of having to think, "what can be said *has* been said – not just by every sixteen-year-old sitting their exams, but by some of the greatest minds in history. Why do you think they pick it? Aside from its excellence, Shakespeare's easy to grade because ... there are *right* answers. Tell the exam board what they want to hear, because then it means you've understood the play the way they intended when asking the question."

"Isn't that ... cheating?"

"What do you think exams are?" She squirmed against the marble as he laughed again. "What do you think knowledge is, Jessie? Telekinetic powers and secret societies?"

"Yeah, I'm disappointed my brain didn't swell up to make my head all giant and veiny. I really wanted to make Dot float. Maybe flip a few cars on Mulberry

Lane, like that bald kid from *Stranger Things* on a nosebleed bender." Johnny laughed again, and she could tell she'd got him back on side. "So, you think I could get a C this time?"

"Most definitely. Maybe even a C+."

Jessie snatched her paper off the island and thrust it into her bag. "Chill out, and thanks for letting me use your printer."

"Do you want to print it again with a smaller font?"

"Makes it look like more."

"No, Jessie." Johnny offered a sympathetic smile and a shake of his head. "It really doesn't. And ... can I offer some advice?"

"About Shakespeare?"

"What else?"

Jessie relaxed as much as she could in the stiff environment. She'd take crumbling cottages over living in an Instagram interior design explore page any day.

"It's more of a question." He pulled out his glasses and produced a case from his tatty old messenger bag. A snap of the box, and he whipped out the cloth. "You ever been in love?"

What?

"What?"

He crammed his glasses on, blushing immediately.

"It's relevant to Shakespeare, I promise. I thought I had experienced love when I wrote my Shakespeare papers, and I think it helped. It was different, but I loved Leah back then, too."

"I always thought you used to fancy my mum."

"Oh." More blush, and lots of it. "I did. That came later. After Leah left. We actually went on a date. Your mum and me, I mean. When she came back to the village."

Jessie had heard the story from her mum's point of view. Apparently, Johnny had wasted little time after her return following her first marriage hitting the rocks. Despite his best efforts, Julia couldn't see beyond the very good friend he'd been to her in school. The way Johnny used to look at Julia had changed around the time Barker proposed – Jessie's first Christmas in Peridale, and her first as part of Peridale's own *Addams Family*. Jessie had seen the heartbreak in Johnny's eyes when he found out, even if no one else had noticed.

And maybe there was still a shadow of it across the island, but he blinked, adjusted his glasses, and looked up expectantly at Jessie.

"Yes," she replied, remembering his question. "Twice."

"I know about Billy, that lad you used to see from Fern Moore. What happened to him?"

Jessie smiled, but it faded when she remembered what had happened when she called her ex-boyfriend at Johnny's autumn wedding. "Oh, he erm – left to join the army, didn't he. I haven't heard from him in a while. He's ... changed his number."

Johnny clicked his fingers in her face, and she was sure her eyes crossed as she stared down her nose at them. "*That* right there. That look in your eyes. Well, not *that* look. Now you're just pulling faces." Jessie put away her stuck-out tongue and uncrossed her eyes, and Johnny said, "It didn't work out, but there's a flash of *what if* in your eyes. In your heart. Isn't there?"

"All right, Johnny. Chill out."

"Sometimes I wonder what would have happened if your mum and I ended up together," he admitted in a voice barely above a whisper, even though the kitchen was empty. "But your mum was right. We made better friends, and it all worked out for the best, didn't it?" He thought for a moment before clearing his throat. "My point is, you need to put yourself in the shoes of that girl who first fell in love with Billy. How old were you?"

Jessie shrank against the marble and wished it would swallow her up. Summer days with Billy all over the village flickered through her mind like a film she knew better than any other. She'd found out that he'd changed his number after too many espresso martinis at a party filled with couples celebrating love. She'd just applied to college, so Billy went to the back of her mind so she could enjoy the rest of the wedding, which she did. She danced with Percy until his hip hurt and taught the twins how to do the *Cha-Cha Slide*.

The morning after the night before, however…

"Can I have a drink?"

Jessie grabbed a glass from the strainer and filled it at the sink. Above the new garden – which resembled the posh geometric displays with fake grass and perfect pebble borders at garden centres – the clouds were a suffocating blanket.

It wasn't like she still loved Billy.

Not really.

Not like that.

She'd ended things two months before her nineteenth birthday, and she was twenty-one next month. Two years and one month, and yet still, a lifetime had passed from the days of listening to Billy talking about *his* plans for *their* future.

Marriage.

Kids.

Constantly.

They'd still been kids.

Jessie still felt like a kid, especially when people were laughing and head-scratching at her work. She'd thought Billy going off to join the army was an overreaction. He'd threatened to do it every time she suggested they needed space, that things were going too fast, that they were too young to get so serious. She'd even tried to break up with him around the time of Barker's birthday party disaster at Wellington Heights, back when it was still a manor and owned by the Wellingtons.

But the crying.

And the texts.

And the calls.

Him trying to move into her new flat above the post office.

And then, no more...

Jessie had sent him off with a hug, told him she was proud of him, and promised they'd stay friends and keep in touch. It wasn't as if she'd stopped liking him, no matter how wrong they'd ended up being for each other. *So, why'd he change his number and drop off the face of the planet?*

"Sixteen," she answered, turning back to Johnny after a final sip of water. She tossed out the rest and put the glass back where she'd found it. "I never thought I'd fall in love, but he was such an idiot, I couldn't help it."

"Well, imagine if he was Romeo," he said, turning off the tap she hadn't realised she'd left dripping. "The answers you seek lie with *that* Jessie. I remember her in her baggy clothes and Doc Martens, constantly hiding in her hoody. She wasn't Juliet, maybe, but imagine if Julia and Barker had tried to keep you and Billy apart."

"Barker warned me off him like ... ten times. He was a detective, and, in his eyes, Billy was a Fern Moore layabout."

"But imagine he proactively stood in your way and *really* hated Billy's parents."

"Barker put Billy's dad behind bars for a murder he didn't commit ... and then accused him of murder again the second he got out. Crikey, Johnny, don't you read the paper?"

"Yes, and *your* family are starting to feel like *The Kardashians* of Peridale, what with the frequency you appear in those pages. I'll be glad to write about something else at my new job."

"I like to think we're more *The Addams Family*. Have you met Dot? She dresses like the ghost of a Victorian school teacher, and – Actually, now that you mention it, there is something of a Kris Jenner about her. Does that mean Julia is Kim and ... and *The Kardashians*, Johnny? Really?"

"What?" He shrugged, pushing up his glasses. "Leah watches it."

Of course she does, Jessie thought, looking around

the house, concealing her judgement of that soup-brained show. She'd accidentally binge-watched two seasons of it on a plane before snapping to her senses. Johnny's analysis wasn't far off. Dot had the box of clippings to prove it. She'd pulled it out as recently as New Year's Eve, after one too many glasses of sherry.

Before Johnny continued to dig all the way to the tales of her second love, Jessie thanked him for his pointers, shouldered her bag, and left. She didn't have time to get into what had happened with Stefan during her time in Berlin. Now that he was on her mind, she realised she still hadn't told Julia about him.

Or anyone in Peridale, for that matter.

Maybe she never would.

It wasn't like Stefan would ever turn up.

Jessie's heart fluttered as she remembered the smile that had caught her off-guard across the bar that night. The filament lights had lit up his eyes filled with honey flecks, like Nadia's. Maybe that's why Jessie had noticed them. And maybe she didn't need to think about Billy after all. Alfie had stood between her and Stefan – but that's what she got for falling in love with one of her brother's friends.

Their short-lived romance hadn't ended with poison and daggers, but her heart hadn't known the difference for a while. She hadn't been able to show it, either, especially after she promised Alfie that she wouldn't bring it up again once they left Germany.

Why didn't I ask Stefan for his number?

Jessie pushed him to the back of her mind.

It wasn't like she hadn't had practice.

"Hey," Alfie said when he answered the phone; he sounded like he was in a good mood. She settled behind the wheel of her car, glancing in the rear-view as someone from the estate agent added a SOLD banner to the sign. "Guess where I am!"

"Well, when we spoke last week, you told me you'd just signed a contract for a six-month position on that farm in South Africa, so … not there?"

"Arches National Park, Utah!"

When it came to travelling, Alfie had ants in his pants.

"You're in the States?"

"Imagine Tatooine from *Star Wars*, but with green trees." Alfie had made her watch the whole series on one leg of their plane journeys, and each movie had left her with more questions than answers. She wondered if Mrs Hardy's alien was more Chewbacca or Yoda. "Anyway, who cares about contracts when you can hop on a plane? Let me show you. I've met some new friends, and we're touring the parks together in a fleet of RVs. See?"

The video flashed onto the screen, and she was

comforted to see her brother grinning at her. He'd changed his lip ring from black to gold, and a different girl was draped around his tattooed neck. Blonde. The last had been a redhead. Alfie certainly didn't have a type. At least, not if his half a dozen travel romances – to her one Berlin fling – in as many months were anything to judge by. And he'd sworn each girl was 'the one' every time, too.

Alfie didn't introduce the sleepy blonde, and Jessie didn't ask.

"Having fun?"

"Always. What's up?"

Jessie wondered if she should keep it casual, but she still had a Shakespeare paper to finish. She couldn't ask about Stefan, not if she wanted to go to college in a good mood, but she could ask about Billy. Alfie and Billy had worked together in that builder's yard, and Jessie felt a pang of regret for that era of her life being a blip already two years behind her. She'd been younger and more naive, but why did every memory from that time have such a rosy glow? Shakespeare hadn't been around to bother her back then, but it was more than that.

"Don't suppose you have a current number for Billy?"

"No different than the one I had when we were all still in Peridale." He curled his lips down and leaned away from the log he was leaning on. Behind him, a burning red disc scorched the horizon, but he hadn't seemed to notice. It did look like Tatooine, and it beat Jessie's grey day. "We just … lost touch. Is his mum still in Fern Moore?"

"No." Jessie had asked around for him at the café in Fern Moore when she'd helped Barker on a case; she'd noticed they were all working in different lanes this time. "It's nothing. I just wanted a catchup. I'll let you get back to your sunrise. It looks like it's going to be a good one. Can't say the same about the one I saw here this morning."

"Up early, meditating like I showed you?"

"Something like that. Have a good one."

"Love you, sis."

"Love you."

Jessie hung up. For all his talk, she knew Alfie wasn't up early to meditate. By the dark circles beneath his usually sparkling eyes, he hadn't gone to sleep at all. He'd stopped asking if she would be joining him on the road again a while ago, and she'd stopped asking when he was returning to Peridale, a place he talked about as being more and more in the same mists of time that had swallowed Billy.

Travelling had been a blast, but seven months back in Peridale was enough for Jessie to know she'd got what she wanted from it. She didn't need to wonder if she was a different person because she'd never been gladder to be exactly where she was, even if she wasn't in the mood for being pushed by Veronica today.

"If there's anyone listening out there," Jessie said as she reversed up the lane towards Peridale Farm, her arm over the back of the chair her backpack was taking up, "please let today be the day I get my first C."

In his shed at the allotment, Barker struck the first heavy key on the typewriter.

C

H

T

P

He reached out for the backspace key that wasn't to be found on the vintage typewriter he'd bought from the antique shop on Mulberry Lane. How he'd written his first book on it, he didn't know, but he'd got too used to his laptop again since the switch to private investigation. He knew the old thing was an indulgence, but he loved the sound, and he didn't need to plug it in.

"Barker, are we all right to carry on?" Dot asked, waving high above her head from under her sun hat, despite the clouds. He gave her a thumbs up. "What are you doing in there, anyway?"

"Just some work."

No mistakes.

He ripped out the paper and rolled in a fresh sheet. Okay, so 'no mistakes' would be impossible on a typewriter, but not in the heading, at least.

C

H

"Barker?"

Q

"Yes, Dot?" Barker pushed forward a smile as Dot poked her head through the open window. She didn't look down at what he was doing; her eyes were trained on the back of the allotment. "What is it?"

"People are arguing on the other side of the metal sheets."

Barker weaved through the beds of planted seeds and the cane structures Dot and Percy had been working on all morning. They'd been waiting there with the dogs before he'd shown up with the typewriter.

"Something about a ring," Percy mouthed, tapping his wedding finger. "She's rather upset."

"Aren't you going to *say* anything?" There was no mistaking Coral's voice, and she *was* upset. "I *know* you took it. I'm not going to tell anyone, just admit it to *me* ... for Henry's sake ..."

Barker held his breath as footsteps rushed off. He leaned up against the fence, looking for any way to peer through. If only he'd inherited the allotment with the gaps in the slats. He pushed a little too hard, the corrugated sheet buckled forward, and the sound bounced back at him after it hit the red wall. Two bolts at the top, none at the bottom. He poked his head through the gap, but Coral was already far down the path, marching towards her cottage, and whoever she'd been speaking to was long gone.

"Did you see them?" Barker asked Percy. "Did they say anything else?"

"I'm afraid not, chap. Is it important?"

"Maybe."

"Explains how they got the body in," Dot announced, brushing off her hands as she followed Percy back to their planting.

The broken fence did explain how the body got in with the carrots. And after finding out the time and date of Henry's death, Barker was certain whoever killed Coral's son had to have been at the launch party for Henderson Place.

Did he die for a ring?

"Are you two fine on your own?"

"As dandy," Percy said as he covered yet another

seed with soil. "Off you trot. Here, Dot, go and ask Martha if she wants to pop 'round for tea again, and see if Patrick down the way has that wheelbarrow he borrowed."

Following Dot as she went to talk with the friends he hadn't had the time to make yet, Barker set off towards Coral's cottage. The red brick wall of Henderson Place pulled him in.

There must be an easy way over it.

Barker needed to find out who had been on that guestlist, and the man he should have spent his morning looking for was just the person who would know.

9

"Every time," Sue grumbled as she pulled onto the road leading into Henderson Place. "I tell them to scatter the parking, but they bunch up right outside the house of whoever's hosting the meeting."

Julia had followed Sue's lead by not saying much during their drive from the café, but now that her sister had spoken, every statement sounded a thousand alarm bells.

Who were they trying to fool with scattered parking? And who were 'they' anyway?

Julia had tried to drag the answers from her sister on the drive over before each had sworn their separate vows of silence. The rolling hills of the Cotswolds countryside were rather beautiful, even on overcast days. Like it had done each time she'd driven over to the place that used to be a buffer between the two villages, Henderson Place smacked her in the face like a giant red brick as they approached it.

"Oh, what now?" Sue muttered, swinging the car into a parking space in such a smooth and swift parallel park that Julia didn't have time to hold her breath before the engine was off. Every second with Sue was like sprinting away from a fire, and the fire was happening on her doorstep. "If Sharon's trying to get her daughter in again, I'm going to—"

Julia's ears pricked up at the possibility of finally getting an answer to something. "Sharon Foreman, Henry's sister?"

Sue shot a sideways glance as she popped off her seatbelt. "Yeah, her. And it's Sharon Henderson. She kept the name and graciously accepted the key to Number One, Henderson Place in the divorce. That's their daughter, Abbie Henderson. A brat, if you ask me. She's going to inherit it all one day and knows it. Crashed our New Year's Eve party a drunk, emotional wreck, but like I said then, if there's ever a night for making a fool of yourself, it's that one. We can't be too careful. There have been whispers of a mole."

Abbie was a girl somewhere about Jessie's age, more interested in her phone than whatever was causing the tension on the doorstep, but that wasn't where Julia's eyes lingered. She'd seen Coral about and looked up pictures of Henry online. Given their living situations, she'd expected some differences between the family members, but she hadn't expected Sharon to be such a statuesque beauty.

Sharon's hair was slicked into the perfect Hollywood waves Julia had never figured out, and her leather pencil skirt and silk blouse hugged her obviously exercised shape. Her calves were as toned as polished bowling pins carved from the same marble as Sue's kitchen, balanced on shoes too high for noon.

"Do you know her?" Julia asked.

"Sort of," Sue said, fingers clasping the handle and her eyes still on her front door. "I think I need to sort this. Jenny is too much of a pushover, and the rules are clear."

"Rules for what?"

"You'll—"

"See?" Julia asked, yanking off the seatbelt as Sue jogged to her front door. "I'd get more answers asking Evelyn and the tea leaves."

Julia joined them at the door just as Abbie snatched her hood up to leave.

"Abigail, you'll need the keys if you're going behind the gates," Sharon called, her voice as slick and refined as her look. She snapped open a small bag and tossed something silver just in time for Abbie to turn and grab it. "And if you see your father, tell him that yes, I will meet him for dinner, but he'll have to come to my place because I'm not going near that new pet of his."

"Aww. Cat or dog?" Jenny asked, her cheeks pricking up.

"Girlfriend." Sharon's bag snapped shut, and she recomposed herself into an even tauter position. "And I'm due in theatre in thirty, so shall we get started? Who's taking this? Has Nadia found her voice yet?"

"She's not here," Jenny whispered in a gossipy tone. "Went home last minute and hasn't come back. It's quite a trek up to the gates, so best not to wait for her, eh? I know some of the girls are late for shift as it is. Who's leading?"

Sharon checked her smartwatch. "I will, but it'll have to be a short one."

"No, it's all right." Sue stepped forward, holding the door open for Julia, though Sharon slipped in first. "If Nadia's Number One now, then that makes me Number Two. Julia, we don't usually let outsiders in, so you'll be better watching from the back."

"Watching *what* from the back?" Julia grabbed her sister's arm as her ears tuned into what sounded like her full café on the other side of the kitchen door.

"Tell me what's going on, Sue. What are you Number Two of?"

Sue's eyes flickered, and a smile broke through, though not enough to erase the fear Julia sensed deep inside her sister. "Oh, Julia. There's so much I haven't told you. We'll get to that. Right now, it's better if I show you."

Julia let go, and Sue took a moment to compose herself before opening the kitchen door. What Julia saw made her jaw slacken. Countless eyes turned towards them, their gazes going to Sue and then to Julia. She'd never felt more like an outsider. A sea of gold pins glittered back at her, and she noticed one on Sue's jacket. Sharon had one on her handbag, and Julia was sure it was the same one she'd seen on Nadia's headscarf.

What was Gran saying about cults?

"Henry didn't start this, but we wouldn't be here without him," Sue said, addressing Julia as well as the room. "Julia, this is the FUN group. Fed Up Nurses. Don't ask, I didn't pick it. Everyone, this is my sister, Julia. Someone murdered our leader, and if you know anything about Julia, you'll know she's trying to figure out what happened to him. If you have any information, let Julia know at the end of the meeting. For now, we have our halted demonstration to discuss, so we need to find a new window. Any suggestions?"

These nurses were having anything but fun. Standing at the back of the room as she listened to their stories, Julia could feel how much they were ready for a change in their roles; she wanted it for them, too. She'd witnessed the pressures of the stretched health system through Sue for far too long.

It turned out there wasn't much Julia could have done to help Sue, despite her sleepless nights worrying about her little sister. But as Sue strode about, taking suggestions and opening dialogues all over the room, Julia saw a shadow of their gran. Through it all, Sue had found some control in the chaos.

Under her wavering vocal cords, Sue's words came deep from her chest with an unshakeable confidence that made her fellow fed up nurses listen to her.

This Sue was as much a stranger to Julia as the one who'd spat venom in the same kitchen the afternoon before, but maybe they were two sides of the same coin.

Jessie lifted her Converse to see what she'd stepped on as she climbed out of her yellow Mini. She picked up a circular metal object, glancing at the stream of people flooding out of Sue's front door and into the cars. College was closed due to a gas leak, meaning she was yawning thanks to Shakespeare for nothing, but she'd wasted no time following the directions to Henderson Place.

Smooth on one side, with tiny cubes raised at different heights on the other, it resembled a circular QR code that had been scrambled up from a design she couldn't make out. She took a picture with the flash and zoomed right in, but it was like no currency Jessie had ever encountered, and she had a collection pinned to her bedroom wall. Weightier than any coin she'd felt, too. Alfie would have known what it was made of in an instant; he might have even known what it was.

Jessie pocketed her find, looked off to where the road ended, and vowed that she'd get on the other side of those gates before she left. After what she'd overheard at the hospital, she had to. She had it all figured out, and *Romeo and Juliet* had helped her get there.

Squeezing past the last of the flow leaving Sue's house, Jessie found Sue in the kitchen with Julia. She hadn't expected to see her mum, considering the café should have been open, which could only mean one thing. Jessie hoped her mum wasn't giving Melissa a third strike; the writing was on the wall with Melissa as far as Jessie was concerned. Julia was always slower to catch up when feelings were involved. If only she didn't keep falling for their fake interview personalities.

"Did my invite to the housewarming get lost in the post?" Jessie asked, her voice breaking up the hug the siblings were rocking in by the window. "What've I missed?"

"My baby sister being a hero," Julia said, squeezing both of Sue's shoulders. "Trying to make a change in the world."

"You can thank Henry," Sue said, giving Jessie the same puzzled look as when she'd turned up at the hospital. "He taught us how to mobilise, how to plan, how to figure out when our insane schedules aligned so we could meet to talk about these things. We're all so spread out, so we could never get everyone at a meeting."

"That wasn't everyone?"

"About half," Sue said, checking her watch. "And as Henry always said, for a movement, you need mass."

Jessie blinked back her confusion. "Wait, am I following this right? Are you telling me that Sue is in her anarchist era, and all those people are nurses ready to fight for their rights?"

"*Peaceful* demonstrations," Sue corrected in a flash. "What else are we going to do? They're not listening.

Nothing makes a difference. We're told to sit and wait, and when does that ever help? We need to do things to get the word out there *now*, and Henry showed us how."

"Sounds like you knew Henry well," Jessie said.

From Sue's scrunched brow and Julia's sudden head turn, Jessie had hit a nerve that Julia hadn't yet realised was exposed. The scrunch continued, and Sue's bottom lip curled down.

Jessie prepared for a lie.

"Nope, not really." Sue quickly brushed her hair in the mirror, her dark roots as long as the caramel highlights clinging onto the ends. "Enough about all this for one afternoon. Story hour will be finished at the library in half an hour, and I said I'd take the kids to that soft play area that makes them do backflips in the car when they see where we're going. Julia, we can pick up Olivia on the way and see if Katie and Vinnie want to join. I feel like an afternoon of being tortured by toddlers in a place with bad coffee where I can't hear myself think."

And people have kids on purpose?

"Jessie, are you just in the area again?" Sue asked, catching her eye in the mirror. "Joining us?"

"I came for a reason, actually," Jessie said. "I'm entering the Easter hat competition at the fete, and I want something to wear to match, but I haven't really refreshed my wardrobe since I got back. Thought I could have a look through your stuff?"

"Help yourself," Sue said, hooking her thumb down the hallway littered with toys. "I want to catch the end of this story hour. You should hear Neil doing the voices. Never fails to crack me up." It was nice to hear Sue laugh. "Show yourself out, won't you? Door locks behind you."

Jessie patted down the pocket of her denim shorts weighed down by the coin she'd found outside and pulled it out. "Is this yours? Found it at the end of your driveway."

"Abbie must have dropped it." Sue had the disc in her hand and into her pocket before Jessie could think about clenching her palm around it. "Key for the gates to the top six houses. Strange things, aren't they?"

Henderson Place's private quarter had a key, and it had been in Jessie's pocket for minutes. As Jessie waved them off, she wished she'd kept her mouth shut.

Original plan, it was.

Get disguise.

Get behind the wall.

Get evidence that Dr Khan murdered Henry.

Simple.

Jessie texted the picture she'd taken to Johnny, asking *What kind of key looks like this?*, before digging through Sue's wardrobe. The bedroom was as messy as she'd expected for two people with twin toddlers who worked full-time, especially given how many clothes Sue owned. She'd always been the trendier sister, but these styles were the ones Jessie remembered from before her travels. Turning collars, Jessie saw mostly fast-fashion labels. That's who Sue had been when she'd first met her. Obsessed with fad diets and restyling her sister, Julia, who preferred the vintage touch. Even with Sue's lie about not knowing Henry Foreman, Jessie preferred what she was getting to know about this new Super Sue.

A grin spread across Jessie's face when she found what she'd been looking for. Sue's scarf collection. She had one in every colour. At some point, they'd been organised from nude tones through earth tones to bright colours, but enough were out of order that the caramel-coloured one jumped out against green and white polka dots in a flash. The scarf went around her head, and the biggest sunglasses she could find from the carousel on the cluttered vanity went on her nose. Wondering what perfume Nadia would wear, she grabbed one a colour that matched the headscarf. She gagged after two spritzes of something creamy and floral, but it wasn't like the cameras had smell-o-vision.

"Ah! Perfect," Jessie said, plucking blue nurse

scrubs from the washing basket by the door before cramming them over her vest. She looked down at her legs, wondering if she should change into trousers, but the look only needed to work from the neck up. Leaving her backpack in Sue's hallway, Jessie left through the front door.

"Ah, Nadia, isn't it?" Jessie's heart sank but at least she knew the disguise had worked. She dropped her head and veered off as the man approached her. "I was wondering if I could you a few—"

"Johnny?" Jessie interrupted, pulling down her glasses, relieved. "It's me. What are you doing here? You didn't reply to my text."

"Did you one better." He pulled something from his pocket. It wasn't metal, but it was a disc made of plastic with the same cubic bumps. "Sent the picture to a friend of mine at the college, and he was able to figure out the size based on your hand and the distance between your palm and the floor, cross-referencing that with an estimation of weight based on the alloy used and – well, it's an AI-rendered, 3D printed version of that key."

"That quick?"

"And the technology isn't even new." He rolled the white plastic towards the sun, which shone through the white wedge. "But a key like this, I've never seen. I *have* seen the design before."

"What is it?"

"The Henderson family shield rearranged. I'll explain on the walk. While I disapprove of disguises for gaining entry to places, you fooled me."

"Keep your head down, and whoever's on the other side of that camera might think you're Dr Khan," she said, looping her arm through his as they sped up the road between the green bushes. "If this key works, and if I'm right, I think we're about to close this case."

"What? How?"

"I think Nadia and Henry were teenage sweethearts, and I think she still loved him. According to my dad, Henry died the day *this* place opened. Dr Khan would have been here."

"As were quite a few people," Johnny pointed out, "but if you're alluding to Shakespeare right now, you might be more on the nose than you think. The police released a statement an hour ago to confirm the time of death, but they included the cause, too. Henry Foreman died of a prescription drug overdose, and judging by how sloppily he was buried, our Romeo didn't take the poison voluntarily."

Then that settled it.

Of course it was Dr Khan.

He could get pills easier than anyone.

Jessie snatched the key from Johnny and sped up,

tightening her grip on his arm, and bowing her head lower as they walked towards the cameras.

This couldn't go wrong.

She wasn't leaving Henderson Place without something to prove it.

Barker checked his phone, but still no text from Detective Inspector Laura Moyes. He'd been surprised when she'd asked to meet him in the River Lounge. It had once been the only bar in Riverswick village, but now there was a row of them in the old factory part of the village, and restaurants too. Barker couldn't believe he could get sushi so close to his doorstep so deep in the countryside these days.

"Traffic," Moyes said as she slid into the booth beside Barker. "You should have ordered."

Barker slid the drinks menu over to the shattered detective as she sank into the rich purple velvet. He suspected this was the first time she'd sat down all day. In her message, Moyes had said that there'd been developments, but he knew he wouldn't get anything without giving first.

"There *is* some kind of ring," Barker confirmed, deciding to start with the positives. "Coral did avoid the question, but she isn't the best liar. Couldn't hide how much she hated her daughter."

"Sounds like my mother," Moyes said, slapping the menu. "Well, it's too early for cocktails, so how about coffee? It's not so bad, though it's about triple what your wife charges."

"Is that why you picked Riverswick over Peridale for your transfer?"

Moyes gave him a knowing smile before ordering two coffees at the bar. She waited for them, making Barker sit on his hands to resist drumming his fingers on the table as he wondered what advancements there'd been. He still hadn't seen sight nor sound of Phil Henderson, though he had a picture of him saved on his phone. He pulled it out. If he lived at Henderson Place, there was no saying he couldn't be among the mid-afternoon patrons enjoying the food offerings at the lounge.

Phil Henderson was in his mid-to-late-fifties, bald, and alarmingly red across his nose and bloated cheeks. He had the world's pearliest smile, which he showed off in every picture. From Barker's search online, it didn't seem like the man was ever photographed out of a suit, albeit one always slightly too small for him. It looked like he was trying to force a more relaxed-looking body into one he didn't have;

the guy either needed to lose half a stone or buy a bigger suit.

"Didn't know if you took milk, so I didn't ask," she said, sliding him the black coffee, how he drank it anyway. "So, you think Coral could have killed her son? Did she mention that she didn't even attempt to speak to him in the two weeks after his death?"

"Wasn't he technically missing then?"

"Never reported, but according to the sister, Sharon, it wasn't unusual for Henry to get swept up by a new cause in a new town. He was always flitting off and coming back when it suited him. Coral never leaves the place, so she'd always stay."

"Two weeks without calls or texts didn't alarm her?"

"According to Sharon," Moyes said, pausing to blow on the hot surface of the coffee, "mother and son weren't on the best speaking terms in the months before his death. She's a lot more forthcoming than her mother, I'll say that. Paints quite a different picture than Coral, who didn't have a bad word to say about Henry."

"Guilt," Barker thought aloud. "Overcorrection."

"Guilt about murder? Or about not speaking to her son before his murder?"

"Time will tell. These developments?"

Moyes smirked. "I'm the one with the badge

around here. Don't go forgetting that. You made your choice, Brown. But there's been a couple. Now that we know Henry Foreman was murdered the night of the launch party and buried in the hours following, we've been able to narrow down our suspects. We've been trying to focus on what's going on here, but all the friends Henry ever made have been calling in to tell us about every tycoon he's got on the wrong side of."

"Phil Henderson being one." Barker drank, but it was still far too hot and scalded his tongue. "Phil and Henry would have been brothers-in-law once upon a time, but if Henry went as far as to glue himself to the floor outside Phil's development, I'll guess they weren't on each other's Christmas card lists anymore. Anything on him?"

"Ah, Phil Henderson," she said, lowering her voice. "Have you heard of Greg Morgan, our local Member of Parliament?" Barker nodded at this, the second time hearing the name in as many days. "Well, he's not involved in *this* case. Not directly, at least. We've been looking into Phil, and it seems he cut every corner possible when building this place. There were investigations and reviews, but someone high up has made it their job to let every sketchy development go ahead around here lately."

"I heard Wellington Heights aren't selling."

"No, but you'll never guess who cut the ribbon at

the opening ceremony." Moyes lifted her brows, and he knew it had to be Greg Morgan. "I almost bought one, but my gut told me not to. They look nice, but I don't know. That place gives me the creeps."

"Best to stay away," Barker said. "So, if you throw money at Greg Morgan, he catches it?"

"Even those fancy glass art projects aren't up to scratch," she continued with a nod before letting out an impressed whistle. "Have you seen them, by the way?"

"Only in pictures."

"Well, they're like nothing I've ever seen," she said, even lower. "But two are empty because they didn't pass the health and safety checks. Goes all the way down to the foundations, according to my information, and Phil isn't one for stumping up each when he doesn't need to."

"How do you know all of this?"

"Because about a week ago, an anonymous source posted a folder as thick as those rotting Yellow Pages in Coral's house to Peridale's station. They couldn't trace who sent it, but whoever it was had been following the money. Whether or not Phil Henderson killed Henry, he won't be a free man for long if these houses start to fall down, let's say that. Your sister-in-law lives there, right?"

Barker nodded, too caught up on the fact he'd

been right to suspect that James Jacobson had thrown money at the Council during the library fiasco. He'd had no way to prove it, but like Moyes had said, Greg Morgan wasn't involved in this case directly.

"You think Henry sent the folder?"

"At first, but by then, Henry had been dead for a week."

"He could have had someone else send it for him if he was killed? Sounds like a pretty organised and motivated guy."

Moyes' eyes lit up, and he was glad he had something to offer, though she didn't acknowledge it out loud. "So, you think Phil Henderson killed his ex-brother-in-law too? Wouldn't it have made more sense to get him out of the way *before* the place was built?"

"Not if Henry was the one to gather that information. Surely, he'd have taken it to Phil first, to threaten him? Phil had some tablets on him, had Henry ingest them somehow, snuck through the first fence he came across that gave way, and buried him. Any idea if he was disturbed?"

"No witnesses have said they saw anything untoward that night, and there were more people in the area than usual, thanks to the party. But good theory, Brown. There is something else. The pills that killed Henry, they were painkillers. The strong stuff. They make you feel sick as a dog and out of it half the time." She went to sip her coffee but paused, and her gaze drifted briefly. "I looked at Coral's records because I noticed she's hiding a limp in her walk. She had a knee replacement last year. Wore it all the way down to the cartilage and carried on anyway, insisting she didn't want to be cut open. I only know this because she attacked a doctor at the hospital when he tried to prep her for surgery. He pressed charges, which he later dropped, and she eventually couldn't take the pain anymore. Following the operation, they prescribed her a course of the exact stuff that killed her son."

"They wouldn't have prescribed her a long course after an operation, surely?"

DI Moyes shook her head. "That's assuming she took any of them at all. There's nothing to say she didn't squirrel them away. She didn't want surgery, lives like a Luddite in the forest, and only eats food she grows. You know she offered me some chicken for lunch? Said she was about to catch and pluck one so it would be fresh."

"Think she might have been trying to scare you away. Or maybe she didn't like me that much," Barker said, glancing at Moyes' coffee as he sipped his own; he remembered that rushed feeling, even on breaks, all too well. "So much for being handsome."

DI Moyes bit her lip, her head dipping while her brows rose.

"You made that up, didn't you?"

Moyes shrugged casually. "Worked, didn't it? You don't get to this rank without knowing how to massage an ego, you should know that. Consider it a prank on a new friend."

"So, we're friends now?"

"I need allies," she said, scanning the bar. "I'm new in the area. Besides, my girlfriend is your wife's bestie, which makes us..."

"Spouses-of-friends-in-law?"

He could tell she was cringing at his 'dad joke' sense of humour, but at least she laughed. Moyes wouldn't make the worst ally, especially since he'd lost his contact at Peridale's station.

"So, is Roxy the reason you moved to—"

"Speaking of friends," Moyes interrupted, louder, while shimmying in. "I never met the man, but I've been hearing rumours. Isn't that John Christie over there?"

"Probably. He was still crawling bars after his divorce, the last I heard, but—"

"He's not crawling, he's working here." She grabbed Barker's chin and jerked it towards the door. "That bouncer there."

Barker squinted, and sure enough, there was John

Christie in a black uniform with a badge on an armband. The man who'd been his first detective sergeant when he'd arrived in the village, and who'd taken over his detective inspector role after his retirement, was now a bouncer at River Lounge. The higher-ups must have called every station in the county to stop him from getting another police job somewhere.

"Heard whispers you two had a bromance going on?"

"Consider it ended," Barker said, draining his coffee. "I didn't recognise him in the new uniform, but he will have noticed, and he ignored me." He put the cup down. "Just like he ignored my Happy New Year text. What can you do? He blames Julia for getting him fired."

"Over the Electric Fury case? For Julia's sake, since we're spouses-of-friends-in-law now, fumbling that festival murder case wasn't the whole reason he was fired. It was simply the nail in the coffin. He was under review, and they were waiting." Moyes leaned in closer, cupping her hand to Barker's ear. "And you definitely didn't hear this from me, but a little birdy told me the chief is considering trying to lure you back to the profession."

Barker's heart sank to the pit of his stomach, which was flipping at the same time.

"What?"

"Yes, I'm not quite sure why either," she said, tilting her head as she looked him up and down. "But as I said, you didn't hear that from—" Her phone cut her off, and she sighed as she pulled it from her jacket. "I put it on Do Not Disturb before I came in, which means this can't be good. *Hello?*"

Moyes listened for a fraction of a second before she was out of the booth and summoning Barker to follow. He didn't ask why as he rushed to the door. Moyes was already unlocking her car as she ran across the cobbles. Barker passed John, who was smoking a cigarette outside. He stared at Barker and then right through him like he didn't know him and never had.

Barker would have been more hurt if he hadn't seen it coming. If John couldn't look past blaming Julia, there wasn't much Barker could do. Besides, he'd grown tired of only getting calls whenever John needed a wingman. A decade ago, sure, but now? Barker would take a friendly coffee in the afternoon any day.

"What's going on?" he asked, tugging his seatbelt across as Moyes slapped the emergency siren on the roof of her electric car. "Must be serious if we're making the day-drinkers noise."

"And here I thought I was moving here for a quieter life," she said, setting off at full speed, blue lights swirling and the siren scattering everyone in their path. "Someone's been stabbed, and five guesses where?"

"Does it start with 'Hender' and end in 'son'?"

"Got it in one," Moyes said.

10

"But I'm telling you, I'd trust Sharon to operate on me over anyone," Sue said, not needing to whisper thanks to the suffocating tinnitus fuzz coming from the slew of tiny tots whizzing around them. Julia could somehow hear their stepmother, Katie, squealing along with the kids. "Everyone who's ever worked with Dr Sharon Henderson says the same thing. She's a stone-faced cow, but she's the most devoted, precise surgeon the hospital has. And I know it's sick, but they collect the death-rate data, and I hear whispers on the wind in those hospital corridors as much as you do in the café."

Sue delivered the last line to Olivia with a babble in her voice. Olivia's arms reached out towards the ball pit as they sank into it. Moments later, she sprang free of Julia's grip and flapped her arms like she was going headfirst into the swimming pool with her floaties on. The twins had been stuck to 'Cool Granny Katie' since they'd arrived at the soft play area.

"And what do those winds say?" Julia asked.

"If you're rushed in for emergency surgery and you see Dr Susan Henderson scrubbing in while they put you under, you can drift off knowing your survival chances just went up a few digits. Henry wanted Sharon to be in the group, but he put it to the vote because she'd be the first non-nurse we allowed in. I know surgeons have their issues – porters, doctors, and ambulance drivers, too – but Henry taught us that we needed to focus on a clear message first. That's how he came up with FUN. I fought against it at first, but he said the oxymoron would make a good headline if we ever got there."

Julia picked up on the same thing Jessie must have when she'd questioned Sue earlier. Sue was trying her best to keep her tone flat, but flecks of affection peppered the edges, like they might if Julia were talking about Roxy or Evelyn.

"Were you close with Henry?"

Sue's lip curled, and she shook her head like she had when Jessie had asked the same question. Julia hadn't believed her then, either, and Jessie had rolled her eyes. "We only met on New Year's Eve. Fireworks and drunk people never mix, so A&E is the warzone you'd imagine every year. We have little parties going in the staff rooms all over the hospital. You pop in and out when you're passing one, blow some party poppers, cram some crisps in your mouth, and rush back out. If you're in there at midnight, you're lucky. I managed to sneak away to watch the fireworks on telly, and Nadia and Henry were already in there, so it was just the three of us for the countdown."

Julia flipped Olivia upright after a brave forward face roll. "And what happened? Wasn't this the same night Henry assaulted Nadia's husband?"

"I didn't hear about that until after the fact, so I don't know what happened there. The countdown started, and I started sobbing the second Big Ben rang out the first chime because all I wanted in that moment was to be at home with the kids. I knew the twins wouldn't actually be awake, and knowing Neil, he'd have fallen asleep in front of some history documentary with Bailey's spilling into his lap."

"And what about Henry and Nadia? Did they seem close to you?"

"I'm getting there. So, I pulled myself together by the time the fireworks display really got going. I knew I'd only have a couple of minutes to spare, so I turned to Nadia and Henry to wish them a Happy New Year. I had no idea who Henry was at that moment, mind you, but I looked, and well ... they were kissing each other's faces off. She's married to Dr Khan, and anyone could have walked in, so I cleared my throat. They pulled apart, smiling like two lovesick school kids who'd been caught in the art cupboard. That's when she introduced him as an old friend from school."

"Jessie thought there might be more going on."

"Let's say it didn't look like one of those kisses you give someone on New Year's Eve because you're both alone. Because if that were the case, I'd have taken one at that moment, even with Henry's ponytail. He had a cute smile. They were snogging as long as I was crying, and it took me a second to catch my breath."

"Sounds like they were doing anything *but* coming up for breath." Julia's chest tightened at the thought that one of them was already dead. "So, that's how your group started?"

Sue nodded. "Henry asked why I was upset. He got me talking, and then Nadia was adding on top, and it just snowballed. We spilt our guts about how fed up we were. Nadia had always kept herself to herself, but she was always there at the hospital. That's how it felt, at least. Every hour, every shift. Certain people get reputations for being dependable, and that's what people say about her. Never even complained about her feet, but she was just as annoyed as me. Nothing official happened that night, but before Henry left, he said something like 'See, it only takes sharing your story with the right person to find out your problems aren't *your* problems alone,' and just him saying that bonded us. He returned the next day and said he knew a way to get us into a bigger room with more people with the same problems."

"And a revolution was born."

"*I* didn't want to rock the boat," Sue said, moving in closer, "but Nadia convinced me. She's the silent assassin behind all of this, and with Henry knowing how to push people's buttons so well, we started growing quickly. Believe me, it wasn't difficult. We practically had people…"

Sue's voice drifted off as the unmistakable pitch of Katie's laughter grew closer. Pearl and Dottie zoomed around the corner and into the ball pit before Julia and Sue's baby brother, Vinnie – technically the twins' uncle but only a month older than them – slid in after them. Katie bounced around the corner, red-faced and out of breath. "They never get tired, do they?"

"If only," Sue said. "Join us. The water is lovely."

Julia laughed, though she still had so many more questions for her sister. Sue shook her head slightly. Maybe she didn't trust Katie to keep a lid on it, or perhaps she didn't discuss things when the kids could overhear. Julia looked around for Olivia, and her heart sank when she couldn't find her. Julia's gaze skimmed the top layer of the plastic balls, only to find Olivia grinning up at her with a cheeky little giggle from beneath them.

"Were you hiding from me?"

Olivia laughed as Julia pulled her out. Before Julia could take a relieved breath, projectiles flew at them from all angles.

"What was the vote?" Julia called to Sue above the chaos, hugging Olivia while letting her nieces pelt her. Her phone vibrated in her pocket, buzzing against the plastic. "For Sharon joining?"

"Henry voted first, and then we went one by one. My vote tied it, and Nadia had to break it." Leaning in, Sue whispered, "She thought about it for *five whole days* before she came back with her answer."

"Why did she…" Julia couldn't finish her sentence as she read over the text message that Johnny had sent her. "Sue, we need to go. We need to go *now*. Katie … this isn't something for the kids, can you—"

"Of course. What's happened?"

Julia shook her head.

Not for tiny ears.

Keeping her expression as bright and light as she could, Julia quickly slipped out of the ball pit; it would be better for Katie to explain she'd gone afterwards.

Sue ran to catch up with Julia as she jogged across the car park.

"Julia? What is it?"

Julia could have said, 'You'll see,' but it wasn't the time for jokes. Not the time at all. Swallowing down the lump in her throat, Julia couldn't even look at her sister.

"I'm sorry, Sue, but it's Nadia. She's been stabbed."

Leaning against the red brick wall at the top of Henderson Place, Jessie stared down the road – not that she was looking at the endless rows of red brick houses. Fresh tears came with each blink, and she didn't try to stop them. After what she'd seen at Number Five, she wasn't sure she ever would.

Pushing her Converse away from the wall as the familiar sight of Sue's car appeared at the far end of the road, Jessie looked back through the space where the gates should have been. Johnny was still speaking with DI Moyes.

Jessie had thought Johnny was crazy when he'd started knocking the bricks, pushed flat so the cameras couldn't see. He'd insisted, "People live here, so there needs to be a way in." The key had worked the second it slotted into the secret panel two bricks from the left, six rows up. The cameras buzzed as they turned, and it didn't take them long to encounter who was tracing their journey as they came to a second fence, this time metal.

"We're doomed," Johnny had said, lowering his head, clinging tighter to Jessie with a shaky grip. "Three options. We turn around, I pull out my ID and we go legit, or we carry on with this insane plan."

"We've come this far."

They'd carried on walking to the security box, and all eyes of the half-dozen men dressed in black suits gathered there watched their every move. But Jessie had kept walking, her head tilted down and her lips drawn tight to stop the quivering, dragging Johnny alongside. The second set of gates creaked inwards on their approach, and Jessie nodded politely, like Nadia had done to her when they'd passed in the corridors.

Blinking back more tears, Jessie tried to listen to what Johnny and DI Moyes were talking about, but the line of trees muffled everything but the sound of Sue's engine coming up the never-ending road. Maybe he was grilling the DI for details for the paper or begging not to be arrested for their forged entry.

Would they care, considering what we found?

"Jessie?" Julia ran at her the second Sue stopped the car. "What happened?"

"Oh, Mum, it was horrible," she said, falling into

Julia's arms as more tears burst forth. "Nadia was lying there in the entrance hall, covered in blood. Her middle ... she'd been stabbed with something. I ... couldn't stop screaming, Mum. I was so angry. It's *him*. It *has* to be *him*."

"I assume you're talking about Dr Adnan Khan?" DI Moyes said as she strode out, hands in her pockets, with Johnny at her heels. "Johnny told me your theory, and that you allegedly overheard him berating Nadia in a cubicle about a comment at a party?"

"There's nothing alleged about it," Jessie said, pulling away from Julia and finding her feet for the first time since the police had dragged her out of the house. "I know it doesn't sound like much, but it was his tone. The way he was twisting everything she said. She didn't stand a chance, it was just ... wrong. I should have said something then. I should have smacked him, or ... or something ... and ... and locked him in a cupboard, and this might not have happened."

"And you'd have been arrested. Dr Khan would have pressed charges, and he'd have won." DI Moyes paused to sigh as she moved out of the road to let the ambulance pass. "Because you're right, what you overheard doesn't sound like much, and it would be your word against his."

The ambulance swerved around Sue's slapdash

parking job and set off down the road. At the back row of houses, the sirens kicked in.

"Maybe not the only word against his," DI Moyes said with a smile. "There's still hope for Nadia. And I don't disbelieve you, Jessie, but it's still circumstantial evidence. That said, I have read Henry Foreman's statement from New Year's Eve, after he was arrested for assaulting Dr Khan. Henry didn't allege the same as you, he alleged worse. Dr Khan denied the accusations and pressed charges for the punch. Nadia refused to give any statement at all." DI Moyes paused, looking around. "Where's Barker? He came with me."

"He went this way," Johnny said, setting off along the right side of the wall. "Said he would check the allotments to see if anyone was hiding."

DI Moyes sighed again. "This is why you don't take civilians to crime scenes."

As they all set off in a line following Johnny, Jessie watched the ambulance turn off at the end of the road. She willed those sirens to stay on until they reached the hospital.

Nadia had to live long enough to regret not giving that statement to the police because if she didn't, Jessie was sure it meant Henry had died for nothing.

"Hello?" Barker called out. "Anyone here?"

As he walked down the path between the allotment shacks, he wasn't sure why he was still expecting a response. Most of the gates and doors were shut, and if people were busy planting and potting behind them, they weren't responding to his voice.

Without the case dragging his attention away, he might have made a better first impression on his green-thumbed neighbours ... or even got his hands dirty, for that matter. The longer Barker spent at the allotments, the less clear became the vision of him spread out on a deckchair with a paperback while the vegetables grew themselves.

Rounding the corner at the top of the path, Barker looked up at the sky through the trees as grey clouds loomed closer, already robbing them of the afternoon light. He squinted down the path between the back of the allotments and the red wall, and he wasn't alone.

A figure was staring at him – no, *away* from him, in the distance. No wonder the patrolling officer with the torch hadn't seen Barker under the thick canopy of the trees. Barker thought about pulling out his own torch, but the flash on his phone wouldn't reach that far. The surface of his shoes scuffed the gravel as he sped up, and he halted, expecting the figure to turn around, but they didn't.

They were wearing a suit, judging by the white collar, with a strange tension in their shoulders, like they were holding in a deep breath.

And grunting.

Tiny soft grunts, like someone suppressing hiccoughs.

There was another sound, and it reminded him of staring at the white sheet in the typewriter while Percy had dug out the beds. Maybe he *wasn't* alone in the allotments after all.

But he was.

Barker could feel it, and the sound was coming from ahead. His footsteps hastened as the man dropped to his knees to reveal another figure. Enough light leaked through the trees as the clouds shifted, illuminating a blood-soaked blade as it fell to the path.

Barker had heard *stabbing*, not digging.

He rushed to the man as he keeled to the side. The suit did fit him oddly, but it didn't look as bad in person as it had the pictures on Barker's phone. He swallowed down his guilt, eyes stinging with tears as he tugged at the buttons of the man's tight collar. The button released, and he gasped, but blood soon spotted his gleaming white teeth.

"You're going to be okay," Barker said, pushing down on the man's midsection, trying to staunch the flow. Blood soaked through his fingers, and he tried not to cry out from shock. "Who was it? Who did this to you."

"Shh," he said, lifting his finger up to his face. "Shhhhhh."

Finger still raised, his hand fell to his side before it could reach his lips. The hand landed by his face in a way that looked like he might have just had an idea, a contradiction to the fading life in his eyes as his last breath hissed out to silence as the finger curled.

Barker wouldn't waste his breath calling out for an ambulance, and though he could hear footsteps, he couldn't yet turn around.

Staring into the blank eyes of Phil Henderson, the very man he'd been trying to find all morning, Barker wondered how it was that he'd just witnessed the developer's last moments and why had the man had decided to make his final act one of silencing defiance.

11

"And so, the April showers begin."

Jessie tapped her hand on the stainless-steel island, tearing Barker away from gazing out the window as rain pelted the darkened stone of the café's back yard the following day. "We don't have long. I need to set off to college soon."

Julia finished the pink sticky note she'd been neatly writing and stuck it onto the steel under 'Suspects.' Jessie plucked and re-stuck it under 'Questions,' but Julia moved it back. Barker added his green sticker, also under 'Suspects.'

"I think Sharon is a suspect," Julia said, firming down the twice-peeled, weakened glue. "She's part of the group that her brother led, she would have been at the party that night, and her ex-husband just died on the other side of the wall of the development where they both lived. She also has connections to Nadia, to whom she lives next door."

"Shh," Jessie said, dragging out the sound. "Shhhhhharon?"

Barker repeated the lazy hand action she'd seen him repeat a few times, the distant look returning to his eye. They'd all spent the rest of the day before at home, shaken, confused, and hoping the police would wrap things up by morning. The rain only sweetened the lack of breaking news.

"He was shushing," Barker said. "I saw it. He was telling me to stop. But why would he do that?"

"To protect someone?" Jessie said, slapping down her note before ripping up Julia's again. "Which is why *I* propose Abbie, their daughter. She's probably going to inherit a fat slice now that her dad is dead, so what's to say *she* didn't stab him all those times?"

"Why kill Henry?"

Jessie shrugged, checking the watch. "Maybe she … maybe Henry threatened Phil Henderson with that file like DI Moyes thinks, and … she was listening in? If her father was ruined, she could lose everything, and Nadia knew, and …"

"If you're inventing motives, I can put Sharon under suspects," Julia said, moving her back for the second time. "Her motive can be … jealousy. Barker, you said that Coral clearly favoured her son over Sharon, her firstborn daughter. Abandoned by the sounds of things. I'm sure it won't be hard to find some motives against her ex-husband. Maybe Nadia somehow figured out that Sharon killed Henry?"

"Or Abbie," Jessie posed. "Let's not forget Coral, either. Now that Phil is dead, that knocks a lot of wind out of the 'protest revenge' angle, but there's still this mysterious ring we don't know much about."

"Oh!" Barker slapped the table, the echo reverberating around the silent kitchen. Julia glanced at the clock. Five minutes to go. "With everything going on, I forgot about that. I was with Dot and Percy at the allotment, and we overheard Coral telling *someone* she knew it was them who'd taken the ring. She just wanted them to confess to her. Didn't get a look at who it was."

"You also said it looked like whoever stabbed Phil ran off towards her house."

"Down a path that cuts off in a dozen directions," he said with a hint of defensiveness. "I do want to speak to Coral again, and find out about the ring. She hated Phil Henderson to the core, so it's not difficult to imagine her stabbing him."

Jessie gulped, and Julia knew she hadn't yet been able to shake the image of Nadia from her mind. She wished she could take it away. At least Nadia was alive;

Julia had already called the ward twice using the direct number Sue had provided.

"Mum, I assume you want to dig further into Sharon." Jessie slapped down her final post-it – 'Dr Khan' written big enough to fill the square – before slinging her backpack over her shoulder. "I'm going to go digging at the hospital after college. I can't be the only person who has overheard Dr Khan saying or doing something incriminating. Do you think the police are still looking for him?"

Barker offered a shrug and sipped his coffee, "If they've found him, they've kept it quiet. I checked Peridale Chat and nobody's posting about him being arrested. I tried to join Riverswick Chat, but they rejected my application. Apparently, I didn't 'qualify' for their community chat group."

"Turns out the borders are drawn deeper than I thought," Julia said, fastening her apron around her back in a double knot. "Rain and two stabbings in Riverswick on a Tuesday in April? I might as well have stayed in bed, if the body in the carrots is anything to judge by."

Julia looked at the counter filled with the cakes she'd baked.

If only she'd slept in.

She'd arrived early to fill her notepad with all the ideas she'd awoken with after sleeping on the conversation she'd had with Barker after the previous day's shock had worn off. She'd baked more than she knew she'd need, but her mind was never in a more meditative state, ripe for thinking, than when her hands were kneading and whisking.

"So, it's either something to do with a ring," Jessie said, jerking up the zip on her fleece as her eyes darted to the window, "or something to do with romance, and I know where I'm placing my bets. And if you hear anything more about who Henry was as a person, that's important too. I'm still helping Johnny with his profile piece for the paper."

"The nurse group too," Julia said, jotting it down and adding it under 'QUESTIONS.' "Henry was a founding member and one of the only outsiders in the group, aside from his sister. Sue's still holding a lot back. Did you notice—"

"Her lying about knowing Henry well?" Backing through the beads, Jessie nodded. "If they first met on New Year's Eve, and she's been the third tier on the pyramid from the first day, then she's had four months to get to know him. Why act like she didn't?"

"Now that I'm thinking about it, the first time I brought him up, she acted like she barely knew his name," Julia said, almost to herself. "Something to look into. I'll keep checking on Nadia and sending updates. Try not to focus on it too much while you're at college."

"Double maths, science, and then time to find out if my second Shakespeare analysis sucked less than the first, and—"

Jessie spun around. Julia followed her into the café and saw what was on the other side of the door that had stopped Jessie in her tracks. "You need to ask Evelyn who's up there looking out for you," Jessie said, "because, considering that Dad just said they hate each other, that's weird."

Julia couldn't disagree as Jessie walked towards the door behind which Sharon and Coral were waiting. They stood a foot apart, Sharon under an umbrella and Coral braving the rain in only a hat, looking anywhere but at each other.

If Julia hadn't known, she would never have guessed that the polished statue dressed in head-to-toe black was even an acquaintance of the rotund woman who looked as though she'd been plucked from the forest, let alone a direct descendant.

"Snazzy place," Coral said as she lumbered up the step, ignoring the doormat upon which people usually wiped their feet. Despite the compliment, Coral's expression was sour as looked at the smoothly painted walls and neat tables. "We're not together. I just caught a lift. Got one of the chaps at the allotment to find your office, Mr Brown. You didn't leaves me a business card, and I thought you'd want to talks with me again."

"My mistake," Barker said, parting the beads for Coral. "If you'll come down to my office? Let me get that door for you there."

"My hands works, don't they?"

Julia recognised the smile Sharon turned her way. She'd given it to strangers on many occasions as apology for her gran's unfiltered remarks. The café was technically open, but Jessie had been right about someone looking down on them. This was a golden opportunity, and Julia would happily delay her first sale of the day to talk to Sharon. She kept the sign on CLOSED and unclipped the latch of the lock.

"Can I get you a coffee while you wait for your ... for Coral?" Julia asked, hurrying back to the counter. "Maybe some breakfast? A slice of cake? On the house, of course."

Sharon opened her mouth as she scanned the menu, the revolving display case, and then the photographs on the walls. She wrinkled her nose and shook her head, and Julia wasn't sure she'd ever been made to feel so trivial with such a subtle look. Maybe standards were higher over in Riverswick these days, or perhaps they had live-in chefs, maids, and for all Julia knew, court jesters on the other side of the wall.

She still hadn't seen the houses with her own eyes, though if they did have court jesters, she doubted Sharon would laugh. If she could. Her shiny smooth complexion was stretched taut over a face that didn't move much on its own, as carved from marble as her bowling-pin calves. If Julia used SPF Factor 50, Sharon must have been able to afford the extra-special Factor 5000.

"Actually," Sharon said, sighing to herself as though she'd just lost some internal battle while Julia made herself a cup of tea, "my mother was correct. We are here separately. I came on Sue's recommendation." She paused and wrinkled her nose again. "They've released my brother's body, and my mother wants to have him cremated as soon as possible, but she won't pay for a wake, so I offered my home. I called my usual caterers, but they usually need three months' notice. I checked everywhere in Riverswick. No one there can help me, either. Sue said that you'd be ... available."

Julia blinked more than she'd blinked in her life, wondering if she should give in to her quivering muscles and let the scowl overtake her customer-facing smile, but she didn't want to lose the golden opportunity shining as brightly as Sharon's domed forehead under the café lights.

"Let me just check," Julia said, flicking through a

book under the counter, sucking the air through her teeth. She was glad she always kept a copy of Barker's novel handy for when tourists visited wanting a signed copy. "If I move this around, and that, and if I pull in some extra staff, and—"

"Look, will a thousand cover it?" Sharon slapped an envelope of cash on the counter with a huff. "Just nibbles and cakes and whatnot. Finger food. The people she'll be inviting won't expect much, so don't stretch yourself."

Catering wasn't a service Julia advertised, but she'd done weddings, funerals, christenings, and even one divorce party over her years running the café. It took being scorched by Sharon's words to realise she'd probably been charging too little. She slid the envelope off the counter and dropped it onto Barker's book. "I'm sure I can pull something together that won't be too ... tasking. How are things over there at the moment?"

"I'm sorry?"

"Henderson Place? After the stabbings yesterday?"

"Oh, yes." Sharon nodded like the events had already slipped her mind. "My poor Phil. I don't know whom he got on the wrong side of this time, but there's no denying that man knew how to make enemies."

"You don't think it's connected to your brother's murder?"

"Why would it be?" Sharon arched a lythe brow. "Henry wasn't stabbed."

"But all three of them were killed or attacked in the same small area. You must think there's something odd about that?"

"Think about it? Why would I want to *think* about it? The police know what they're doing, surely. DI Moyes seems like a competent woman." Her expression shifted minutely towards pity. "Then again, I'm sure you don't have the same trust in your officials over here. I hear Peridale's quite bad for crime?"

Julia returned the arched brow, wondering if Sharon was looking for places to throw in her condescending remarks or if they slipped out naturally whenever she entered the lair of a lesser being across the border. If this was the prevailing attitude in Riverswick these days, maybe Julia's customers' dismissal of their second-hand gossip wasn't so misplaced.

"You know Nadia well," Julia stated, unwilling to give up; she had until Barker was finished talking to Coral. "You're in the FUN group together. Surely, you're upset."

"That it happened to her? Yes." Sharon glanced at

a chair as though considering sitting in it. Instead, she stiffened up even more. She'd barely moved from her position; the statue had entered waiting mode. "But wasting my energy on emotion won't save her. I was in surgery in the theatre next door while the surgeons stitched her back up after her silly suicide attempt, so they are the ones who—"

"Suicide attempt?"

Julia couldn't believe her ears.

"It's one of DI Moyes' latest theories. She's found evidence that Nadia was foolishly having an affair with my brother, and they were spotted by quite a few people being rather intimate at the New Year's Eve party at the hospital. Suicide makes much more sense than pointing the finger at Dr Khan. I can't believe they would try to slander a surgeon's name like that."

Hearing 'New Year's Eve Party' knocked loose something Sue had said when Julia first referred to the scattered parties at the hospital as a single event. They'd just arrived at Sue's house, it had been the first time Julia had seen Sharon, and she'd been trying to get Abbie into a meeting.

"How's Abbie?"

"I'm sorry?"

"Your daughter?"

"Yes, I know to whom you're referring when you

say 'Abbie,' I'm just wondering why you're referring to her. Do you *know* Abigail?"

"No, and I'm sorry if I've crossed a—"

"You have." Sharon's jaw clenched. "But she's as you'd expect. First Henry, and now her father. She'll inherit more money than she can ever spend though, so she'll be fine."

"Money isn't everything."

Sharon's icy glare snapped onto Julia; she'd been avoiding looking directly at her for too long. "I'm not trying to suggest that her father's money will heal her current pain, but it will give her the security she needs. That's all. Are you suggesting something?"

"Not unless there's something to be suggested?" Julia waited for Sharon's expression to crack, but the taut stone didn't move. "I heard Abbie was at the hospital on New Year's Eve, quite upset about something. Henry and Nadia were there too, and you just made it sound like Abbie knew Henry?"

"Is that about her silly crush?" Sharon muttered as though to herself. "She'd probably been drinking. She's young and it was New Year's, what do you expect?"

"What crush?"

"It's nothing."

Silly crush?

If Sue had seen Abbie at the hospital, she must

have been in the same staff room as Henry and Nadia. But surely not...

"Henry's her uncle," Julia thought aloud.

"Technically *not*," Sharon answered quickly. "Like I said, a silly crush. Abigail was already over it by the time he died. Her father was stressed, a lot was going on with the divorce, and—" Sharon looked more flustered than Julia thought she'd ever be capable of. "She's not my biological daughter. Or Phil's, for that matter. He sort of ... inherited her from his previous marriage after his wife died. He was her stepfather, so I was barely her stepmother, but I have promised to take care of her, and..." She was still flustered. "Look, the whole thing was embarrassing for all of us, especially her. It was over before it even set in. She didn't even know Henry was my brother, at first. They kept bumping into each other because she always insisted on using the back entrance to Henderson Place, near those falling-down shacks they call *allotments*. The second I found out, I put a stop to it. It was only ever a one-sided infatuation, anyway. Henry only had eyes for Nadia, and—"

They both jumped as someone tried to get through the locked door. Julia shouldn't have enjoyed seeing Sharon flinch and be caught so off-guard, but it was the most human the woman had seemed since she entered the café.

"*Julia?*" Dot called through the door. "Open up. I can see your shadow."

"Read the sign, Gran."

"You better open this door right now, young lady. This is an *emergency*!"

It always is, Julia thought as she hurried to the door.

Dot burst in, her tablet computer clenched in her fist. No matter how many times they'd told her shaking the thing wouldn't make it connect to the café's Wi-Fi any quicker, she still did it every time. While something buffered on the screen, Dot glanced up at Sharon and the two women sized each other up.

Julia braced herself. *This could get explosive.*

"Look!" Dot cried, gasping as a video started to play. "There they are. And oh no! The police are already there."

Julia stared at the screen, which currently played a feed of the local news from outside the hospital entrance. Hundreds of people with banners were trying to get into the hospital, with almost as many officers in padded riot gear waiting on the other side. Just as many people watched on from the sidelines, and more than one camera pointed at the scene.

"I told them this was a ridiculous idea," Sharon said, snatching the tablet from Dot and turning away from them. "They have no clue what they're doing!

Any cause they had will be ruined now." Sharon shook her head. "I bet it was your sister who sent them charging into battle. She was an emotional wreck when I spoke to her this morning."

"One of her friends was almost murdered yesterday," Dot said, wrenching the tablet back. "And who are you when you're at home, anyway?"

"Sharon Henderson," Julia replied.

"Ah, I've heard about you." Dot looked pleased with herself, nodding as she took the woman in. "Ssssharon, isn't it?"

"Excuse me?"

"And *you*!" Dot cried at Julia. "How come I had to hear about all that crazy stuff happening in Riverswick from Ethel White, of *all* people! Percy and I decide to take *one* day off from the allotment, and all hell breaks loose."

Julia's heart sank when she saw her sister on the screen. She was screaming at the top of her lungs, holding one side of a FAIR HOURS, FAIR PAY banner as a wall of police officers closed around them.

"And once again, we are live from the scenes of a demonstration outside of the doors of the accident and emergency unit that has been causing no end of havoc here this morning." A reporter delivered the lines deadpan down the lens as a camera panned away from the crowd. "Who this group are, we have yet to confirm. Local police have confirmed that they received a tip-off late last night that this unplanned, surprise demonstration would occur here today. Sources are saying they planned to breach the hospital and protest in the wards, and who knows what kind of untold chaos that would have caused. For now, the police seem to have things contained here at the scene. Back to you in the studio, Pete."

In the studio, Pete moved on to a more optimistic story about a local teenager who'd won a national dance competition, and Dot quickly tapped the screen to stop the video playing.

"Did you know Sue had joined a militia, Julia?" Dot demanded. "I told you to check on her! Cults, Julia. Cults!"

"It's not a cult, Gran. They're just protesting – something *you* never need convincing to do, usually. Sharon here is also part of the group."

"I was. They ousted me last night after the incident at Nadia's. They're on edge, and they decided to close ranks after I told them I thought this demonstration was a bad idea and I didn't want any part of it. I'd hoped they'd head my warning. I knew their emotions were running high after what happened, and it seems I was right. Henry wouldn't have done it this way."

"Were you close to your brother?" Julia asked.

Sharon stared blankly, as though considering whether to answer, but Julia saw something soft flicker behind that polished expression. "We had grown closer in recent months, yes, much to my mother's dismay. She tried her best to force us to be exactly like her, which usually turns out one of two ways, as my brother and I demonstrated. You become exactly like your parents."

"Or you rebel," Dot finished for her.

"Exactly. I chose rebellion, my mother chose regression. She always knew I wanted more, and she resented me for it. I got out of her clutches as soon as possible and never looked back. She'll tell people it was her choice to abandon me, but she's the one who never leaves that forest. To be honest, this might be the farthest she's been in years. And yet, still, I drive her here, after all the division she caused, after all her years of trying to drag us back into the past with her." With a sigh, Sharon moved in and, in a lower voice, said, "My mother tells people she inherited that house from her parents, but it's not the truth. I'm not sure if she even has any legal right to be there. Her parents died when she was little, and she had a sort of normal life with her aunt until she married my dad. When he died, her mind snapped. Henry was too little to remember, but I do. We lived in a normal house, she let us go to school, and then ... she stopped trusting everyone, and she stopped trusting certain foods, and then it was what we could watch, or what songs we could listen to, or where we could go and who we could see. She practically kept us prisoner, but she'll lie and say anything to smear my name any chance she gets. There's been trouble in my life every time I let them anywhere near it."

"How do you know she tells people things about you if you don't have anything to do with her?" Dot asked.

"Because my recently deceased ex-husband and my mother had constant run-ins about something as trivial as houses. He did his research on her. He had to figure out how to stop her from causing trouble, but I told him not to waste his time. She was happy to let Henry be the one to pull off all those stunts for her. The poor boy didn't stand a chance. She was never going to let him go. There's no getting through to them. I tried. Henry was the exact same, and now so are his minions. The rest of them, I might understand the risk, but Sue? She'll be lucky to make it out of her suspension after this."

"*Suspension*?" Julia and Dot echoed at once.

"Didn't she mention it?" Sharon's slender neck extended and craned to the side as the back door opened and Coral walked through. "Time to go, Mother. Julia, I'll expect the food at mine by no later than nine on Wednesday. Of course, I assume you and your servers will be in standard full black-tie formal?"

"Standard," Julia replied with a nod, still too stunned by what Sharon had just revealed about Sue's 'time off.' "We'll be there."

"Mother? Are you ready to leave?"

Coral grumbled deep in her throat as she hobbled after Sharon, who couldn't get out of the café and into the rain quickly enough. The café door shut behind them, and Dot's hands went to her hips.

"Sue told *me* she'd finally taken her holiday leave!"

"Me too," Julia replied, pinching the bridge of her nose. "What do we do? Go to the hospital?"

"And get ourselves arrested?"

"Have I missed something?" Barker asked, looking between them.

"FUN are causing a scene at the hospital."

"And the local news aren't reporting a single thing about their cause. It's just word salad to avoid saying that those banners are right." Dot glanced at the window as Sharon's sleek car glided off into the rain. "What a peculiar woman."

"Like mother like daughter then," Barker said, leaning against the counter, arms folded. "You know how we heard Coral trying to get someone to confess to taking the ring?" Dot nodded, and he scratched the side of his head. "She completely denies that it happened. She's finally admitted to the *existence* of a ring, but she insists I must have been mistaken and it wasn't her we overheard."

"Maybe she's protecting someone?" Julia suggested. "What's the significance of the ring?"

"I'm not sure there is any," he admitted. "Coral inherited a diamond ring passed down from her parents that was worth a fortune, and she refused to sell it. Henry came to her and asked if he could pawn it to raise some money for the nurses' cause, but Coral refused. The ring went missing a few days later. She accused Henry, he got upset, and she never saw him again. Their final argument was two weeks before he died. Said she didn't want to tell me the first time I spoke to her because she was too grief-stricken, and she didn't think it was important. I think I believed her, even if she wouldn't admit to being overheard."

"Tell her what stony-face just said," Dot said, nudging Julia's arm. "You might want to start hooking them up to lie detector tests downstairs if you believe her, Barker. Sharon just basically called her mother a two-faced liar."

"Said she invented a backstory," Julia said. "That the move to the forest was some sort of regression after the siblings' father died."

"Oh, right." Barker's brow furrowed as he fixed his eyes on the floor. "In that case, I'll say to you what I'd say if this was still my investigation. I think I have a bias in her favour for the silliest of reasons. It's better if you talk to her next time, Julia. You can see what you make of her."

"What bias?" Dot asked.

Blushing, he said, "She reminds me of my mum, that's all."

"Oh, Barker." Julia placed her hand on his head and rubbed her thumb against his hair; he rarely brought up his mum. "Of course I'll talk to her. I have a few questions to ask her myself. I might try and find her cottage later."

"And I'm off to see if DI Moyes has found anything on the other side of that wall," he said.

"Which reminds me, I've booked us a date with those houses. Either of you free to serve at a funeral service wearing black-tie formal?"

After agreeing that they'd help, Dot and Barker went their separate ways. Alone in the café, Julia couldn't help but let the cold energy left behind by Sharon swirl around in the emptiness.

Sharon hadn't given much away, and yet her distance to the horrors happening on her doorstep was suspicious in itself. Maybe that distance was the sacrifice that came with being one of the area's top surgeons? Whatever her deal was, Julia was sure there was more Sharon wasn't telling her ... and Sharon wasn't the only one. Julia pulled out her phone and opened a new message to Sue: *Just saw you on TV. Do I need to bust you out of jail?*

Julia rested her phone against her chin. She wished she could slice through the noise with the precision she needed to figure out what was going on. The answers could be staring her in the face, and the sooner they came into focus, the sooner she could properly help her sister – her possibly *unemployed* sister.

Phone still in hand, she called the ward to check on Nadia. After what she'd just seen on the news, she needed to hear something good.

12

Jessie darted her eyes at the phone under her desk as the three dots popped up to signify that Johnny was replying. He took his sweet time typing out his message, making her think he was building up to a lengthy explanation of how everything had been solved, but the text message amounted to what she'd been hearing all morning.

Nadia was still fighting for her life.

And her husband was nowhere to be seen.

"*Miss!*" Ben's grating voice pulled Jessie's eyes up, and she realised Veronica had been watching her. Jessie tucked away her phone and returned to reading *To Kill a Mockingbird* ... and something about pouring cement into a hole in a tree? "Miss, look. I'm you, Miss."

Ben twisted around in his seat with that dumb grin, showing off the black glasses he'd drawn around his eyes to match the smaller-than-usual frames Veronica Hilt had picked out for the day. Her outfit was subdued, but maybe she'd dressed to match the dreary weather.

Jessie looked at the lidless pen on Ben's desk and wondered if he knew or cared that he'd used a permanent marker. It'd be worth it for the laugh, right?

Except nobody was laughing.

Even Ben's comedy glasses couldn't pull them away from their phones.

"Very humorous," Veronica said, her tone dull. She didn't patronise him with her usual *well done, clown* smile. "I do hope it washes off, though we'll see tomorrow, won't we?"

"Not coming in."

"You always say that," Jessie found herself saying, "and yet you *always* come in."

The people around Jessie glanced up at her from their phones. Did she not speak much in class? She never answered questions out loud, that was for sure. Ben answered too many, and rarely with anything serious. Maybe Jessie hadn't drawn on glasses to mock a teacher, but a much younger version of her had stuck pens up her nose. She'd stormed out of her fair share of boring English classes, too – if she even bothered turning up in the first place.

In school, everyone had called her Jess, and Jess hadn't cared about much. Hadn't thought there would be much ahead of her. Jess would rather have been put in detention than attempt to read *To Kill a Mockingbird* or go exploring with Shakespeare. Next to the pen, Ben's copy of the book remained unopened.

"That's time, so clear off," Veronica announced, missing out on her usual desk slap. "Bring in your coursework, et cetera, et cetera, you know the rest. Jessika, a word?"

The rest of the class shuffled out, and she heard a couple of "What's wrong with Veronica?" questions as they went.

"Better," Veronica stated, slapping her latest paper on the desk. "A C. Did you have help?"

"Yes. But I think I understood it more in-depth too, and he only gave me pointers and stuff to think about. I wrote it. My friend, Johnny, read over it."

"Johnny Watson?"

"You know him?"

"I knew of whom you were speaking, didn't I?" Clearly, Veronica's coldness wasn't reserved for just Ben today. Something had happened, but a high wall with a spiked fence and a moat filled with sharks told Jessie not to knock on *that* door. Teachers, even when they insisted you called them tutors, never liked that. "You can do better."

"I thought I had?"

Veronica pulled out a satsuma, sat it on the desk, and stared at it as though waiting for it to respond for her. "You understood that Juliet is a prisoner in her family a little better and that her love for Romeo presented an escape for her. I liked how you related the distance their families put between them to present-day long-distance relationships. People are so determined to believe a filtered digital version of a person rather than reality, nowadays. Relating that to how Juliet mirrors Romeo when he speaks as an example of that mirroring and projection was well-handled, too." The compliment did reach Jessie, but the delivery left her feeling like Veronica was digging for gold in a coal mine. "You're still judging her too much by modern standards. You're expecting her to *know* what to do, while somehow both pointing out and neglecting the fact that she is a young woman. You can still do better, so *do* better."

Jessie snatched up the paper and stuffed it in her bag. "I'll give it another go. Are you ... all good, Miss?"

"For the last time, you're not in school."

Veronica picked up the satsuma, and Jessie left

reluctantly. It wasn't like she'd never seen a teacher in a bad mood before – often, in fact – but never Veronica Hilt. She couldn't believe she actually cared about what had happened to a teacher outside of the classroom, but she did. Jessie lingered by the door, gathering the nerve to ask again, when a finger tapped her shoulder. She spun around to see Johnny.

"I'm beginning to think you're stalking me."

"I'm here to kill two birds with one stone," he said, glancing into the classroom, "so don't feel too flattered. So?" He flashed an excited grin. "How did it go?"

"C."

"Hey!" He clapped his hands, looking more excited than Jessie had been. "Not bad. A pass. Well done. Are you proud?"

"Not good enough, apparently." Clutching the straps of her bag, she looked back at Veronica, who still had the satsuma in her hand but wasn't peeling it. "What am I doing here, Johnny? If my best isn't good enough, what's the point?"

"Do *you* think this is the best you can do?"

"What if it is?"

"You've just gone up a whole grade in a few days," he said, laughing in a way that made her feel like she was taking it too seriously; the laugh caught her sideways, and she felt her cheeks flush. "Look, you can do better. Don't let Hilt get to you. She's one of the good ones, trust me. If she's putting pressure on you, it means something."

"She did just mention that she knew you."

"Taught me during my A levels at college," he said. "A different college. We were all a lot younger back then, but she still had those glasses and that fire in her belly. I'm just here to talk to her about something for the paper."

"Consider her fire put out today, but good luck. I need to get to the hospital to check on Nadia."

"There's no change, and don't go yet. Like I said, two birds, one stone." Johnny reached into his messenger bag and dragged out a lanyard. He dangled it before her, twisting an ID badge with a shimmery authentication logo that caught the hall lights. "It can open as many doors as it has shut in your face, but it might be handy. Use with caution. I'll trust you'll know what to do with it."

Johnny dropped the badge into her palm front-side up. She smiled at herself from a picture pulled from her socials. She could tell she was in a retro gaming arcade in Tokyo from the soft pink glow of the neon lights saturating the background. At that point in her travels, she'd already decided that she'd be cutting her country-hopping short, but she hadn't admitted it to herself or Alfie. He'd taken her there to cheer her up when he'd sensed something was on her mind. She won four of five games of *Pac-Man* against him, but she'd been sure he'd let her win.

"Didn't you hear 'could do better'?"

Johnny ignored her. "It's only good until the end of the week because it expires when I do. I can't promise the next editor will give you a shot, but I am leaving a letter of recommendation for you, whether or not you want a job there."

"It's just one C."

"Not because of that, and you know it." He smiled, taking a step nearer to the classroom. Veronica had finally peeled the satsuma, but she was back to staring at it on the desk. "The information you've been getting on Henry Foreman has been really helpful, and your testimony about what you overheard has strengthened the case against Dr Khan."

"It was social media digging, and I was in the right place at the right time."

"The information is only *one* piece. How you interpret it and present it, that's journalism. Have some faith in yourself, Jessie. Your instincts were right. I stopped by the café on the way here, and your mum said Sharon confirmed that Henry only had eyes for Nadia. They might yet prove to be Riverswick's very own Romeo and Juliet."

"You think she could have tried to kill herself?"

"That's what I've been hearing." Backing into the classroom, he leaned forward and, as he went, whispered, "'O happy dagger, this is thy sheath, there rust, and let me die.'"

Comparing the badge in her hand with the weight of *Romeo and Juliet* in her backpack, Jessie took a few ambling steps towards Happy Bean, but she didn't reach the stairs.

No way had Nadia stabbed herself.

And Henry hadn't buried himself, either.

No way.

Somebody else was up to Shakespeare's tricks, and as Johnny had advised when working on her coursework, 'a little tunnel vision can help propel you to the end.' He'd been right. Even if she hadn't mastered finishing her work before midnight, she was finishing.

Can do better, eh?

It was time to see how far a badge with her face, name, and a shiny security sticker from *The Peridale Post* could get her. Maybe they could even glue Adnan Khan to the hot seat she'd helped to put him in.

Jessie set off to the hospital sporting a can-do attitude and her new unearned credentials dangling around her neck. She would finish this by proving she was the one walking down the right tunnel. There was no way she was the only person who'd ever overheard something.

"Great first case, Laura," DI Moyes muttered under her breath. She'd been pacing in and out of the fiery beams of sunlight bleeding through the canopy into Barker's allotment for as long as the sun had been setting on another day of the unsolved case. "So, you're telling me that I have to disregard everything Coral has said because her daughter called her a liar?"

"We've both caught her out in more than her fair share of lies," Barker reminded her. "I was standing right *there* with two witnesses while she was on the other side of that metal talking to someone, and she *still* denied it until she was blue in the face. Sharon claims they had a 'normal' life before her dad died, so you might want to look into that to confirm which of the two we should trust."

"I'll decide what I do for my investigation, thank you," Moyes snapped, glancing at him from the corner of her eye as the pacing slowed. "I'm sorry, it's … my first case here. You know they offered me the Peridale job? Everyone's avoiding it like the plague because there seems to be a curse attached to it."

"I'm not cursed."

"Then I won't tell you what they say about you and your wife at the station." She stopped pacing and perched on the edge of the bed in front of the wooden beams awaiting beanstalks. "I've spent the best part of fifteen years flitting up and down this country like a travelling circus clown, solving pesky crimes that have somehow gone unnoticed for years. I loved it, and I was damn good at it too, but I felt like it was my time to stand still. When the call to slow down came, I listened."

"We have more in common than I thought."

"Except it's not slow, is it?" DI Moyes leaned on her elbows and ran her fingers through her hair; if Barker were the type to carry a hipflask, he'd have offered it. "Three deaths on my patch, all unsolved as of yet, and now you're telling me the one case I thought I was building has lost all kudos until I can prove which of them is a stone-cold liar? Though, as you said, we've both caught Coral out. She still won't admit to receiving a prescription after the knee op, either."

"She's clearly scared of authority."

"I think she wants *us* to be scared of *her*." DI Moyes lifted her finger to show a healing scab. "Old witch stuck a pin in her gate."

Barker held up his matching fading red dot, and

they shared a laugh. The allotment had quietened as the sun finished its journey over the horizon.

"This place needs some streetlights," Barker said. "You'd probably have Coral protesting that the light disturbs the vegetables, but I'd have seen who killed Phil."

DI Moyes pushed herself from the bed by her knee, grunting deep in her throat as she snapped upright. "I love my job. I love my job."

"It really is one of those days."

"Tomorrow's a new one, and I have plenty to get on with. I only came by because I saw Coral and Sharon coming out of your wife's café earlier. I wanted to see what the deal was. The last thing I need is a Julia-shaped spanner in the works."

"Spying on us?"

"I took Roxy out for lunch at River Lounge, Mr Brown," she said, tugging open the gate for herself before he could rush in to do it. "And since you've told me all you know, I will now ask that you stay out of my investigation. Three people are dead, and you proved yourself to be reckless in how you stumbled upon Phil Henderson yesterday."

"It's hardly *all* I know. I have ideas about—"

"I don't need any more half-baked theories, thank you, Mr Brown," Moyes called as she walked towards her car at the top of the path. "I've had everyone from the Superintendent to PC Puglisi filling my head with theories, and what I need right now is a deep tissue massage, a large glass of red, and my thoughts. If you so desperately want to be a detective, you shouldn't have thrown away your job."

DI Moyes left a trail of smoke behind her as she disappeared around the curve of the path. Barker hadn't put her down as a vaping type when they'd first met on the time capsule case, but then, he'd also thought he'd made a friend in the new DI.

He'd fallen for a trick he'd employed himself many times.

False intimacy and flattery loosen tongues; Barker just hadn't expected to be the one on the other side of it.

Idiot.

And she'd been right.

Looking around the allotment, he wondered why he was trying so hard to prove something the police were already all over. He'd waited so long for the keys to his allotment, and he'd tossed it aside like a Christmas present he'd begged all year for and broken by Boxing Day.

Retired or not, the old DI brain was always firing up.

Barker stared at the fresh, crumbly soil of the bed in which he'd first found Henry Foreman on that sunny afternoon. He hadn't had a care in the world other than trying to remember who he used to be. Ironic that while he didn't know who he *currently* was, he did know how the culprit had snuck through the metal fence missing two screws. The hole had been dug using a standard shovel that still hadn't turned up. Whether that was important had yet to be determined.

The state of the burial had seemed important from the moment Barker first examined the crime scene. The rushed job had left the victim on display. PC Puglisi and Barker had drawn the same conclusion at the scene – the person with the shovel must have been disturbed by something and fled.

For two whole weeks, they could have returned to finish what they'd started.

So, why hadn't they?

Perhaps, they hadn't been able to face finishing what they'd started. For the first time in years, Barker thought about his old cat, Millie.

Or more specifically, about Millie's burial in the garden of his childhood home.

Barker's mum had started digging the grave, but she'd been too upset to finish. At eight years old, Barker took the shovel from his mother and finished what she couldn't. If he hadn't been there, she would have finished eventually, maybe later that evening, but

Millie was a cat. A lovely cat who used to curl up above Barker's head in bed.

What if Millie had been Barker, and his mother had murdered *him*?

Impossible to think about.

Not his mum.

But if she *had* half-heartedly buried him in an allotment behind a locked gate, she might have thought she had all the time in the world to return.

It wasn't like the previous holder of the keys to Plot Seven, Tommy, had been around for a while, after all.

Coral had mentioned it on first meeting him.

13

The rain stopped long enough for Julia to watch the scorching sunset burn across the field behind her café before flickering away like a blown-out candle. From almost the moment Julia twisted the lock at the end of the day, the downpour began afresh.

"I don't think it's going to stop any time soon," Sue remarked lazily as she looked out at the darkness. Thunder rumbled somewhere far in the distance. "These April showers are trying to prove why they earned their name. You don't mind if I stick around for a bit longer, do you?"

"Not as long as you keep helping," Julia said, and Sue picked up the batter she'd been whisking before abandoning it to watch the rain. "You used to do that when we were kids. Sit by the window when it was raining, I mean."

Sue pulled up the bowl and whisk and turned out her bottom lip. "Did I? I don't remember. Do you think you'll be able to get everything finished before the funeral?"

"You used to do it for hours. Couldn't pull you away."

"I said I don't remember."

There was a bite to Sue's voice, but Julia decided to drop it. She'd been prickly since she'd turned up, with an air of *please don't go there*, so Julia hadn't. It didn't mean she wasn't desperate to know what was happening. Once upon a time, she'd have been the first person Sue would have called. Now, Julia wasn't even sure if Sue knew that she knew.

"Olivia was already having a sleepover at Dad and Katie's," Julia said. "I might be here all night pulling this together. Do you actually want to help? I hoped Jessie would be around to lend a hand, but she's probably hunkering down with Shakespeare. How many nurses did you say were showing up at the wake tomorrow?"

Sue poured her batter into one of the waiting cake tins as Julia pulled finished fluffy sponges from the steaming oven. "Not sure. A fair few. And are you sure you trust me? You know I'm not the best baker. I never inherited that skill from Mum."

"Mine's as much taught as inherited, but you were never as interested. You always preferred making up worlds with your dolls. You're doing great. It's maths and mixing."

"It's a *little* more than that."

Julia dipped her finger into a fluffed-up meringue mix she planned to turn into some quick and easy bulk Eton Mess pots and offered it to Sue. "Do you think this needs more sugar?"

Sue dipped, licked, and went back for a second dip while the first worked around in her mouth. "Yeah, I'd say so. Is that orange?"

"Satsuma. I've been getting whiffs of them for months for some reason, so I must be craving them."

"Not..." Sue jerked her head down. "Baking a second bun in the oven."

"Absolutely not," Julia answered with a little too much force. "Love motherhood, but it hasn't even come up." She sprinkled more sugar as Sue returned to her whisking, and the same question brewed in reverse. "Are you ...?"

"Also no."

The two of them returned to their tasks in a silence that wouldn't have felt so awkward once upon a time, but it did, and Julia hated it. She hated the situation that was making Sue avoid opening up to her. It wouldn't be the first time; Sue had always been one to drift off to the rainy window. Julia didn't expect Sue to tell her every detail of her life – they had always given each other more space than that – but in times like these, she always hoped Sue would lean on her more.

Even if Sue planned to stay bottled up, Julia couldn't. "How's Nadia doing? Any change? I called a few hours ago. They said she was still stable."

Sue shook her head and said softly, "Can we not talk about it tonight?"

Julia agreed with a nod as she mixed maybe a little too much sugar into the meringue mix, but she couldn't hold her tongue any more than she could stop sprinkling. "Sue, don't get upset."

"Oh, come on Julia, what did—"

"I know about the suspension. I didn't go looking, but Sharon mentioned it. I think she thought we'd know, but—"

"I'm *sure* she thought that," Sue said, thumping the bowl down onto the steel. "Okay, you want to talk about it this badly, Julia? Fine, we can talk about it."

"Sue, it's—"

"No, let's *talk* about it, Julia!" Sue cried, tossing out her hands and fixing her sister with a desperate stare. "That's *exactly* what'll fix things right now. *More* talking. The career to which I've given my time, my sweat, my tears, my entire adult life is now potentially on the line because ... I said 'enough'? Henry said if we made the right noise ... caught the right ears ... we'd be able to *change* things."

"You can."

Sue's shoulders hunched up into a laugh tinged with that dreaded venom. "You know what, I should never have let Henry give me hope that we could actually do something. I thought this was it, Julia. I made my choice. *Fight*. That's what my gut told me to do. How could I be that wrong, Julia? How?"

Julia stared at her sister and tears filled her eyes identical to the ones plumping Sue's bottom lashes. Sue was begging for answers, but the big sister, for all her sleepless nights, had nothing to say.

She'd had bad days at the café, but never like this.

"Take a breath," Julia managed, reaching out. "It's all going to be okay, Sue. We need to figure out a way to—"

"No, Julia." Sue wriggled away and held out both hands. "I'm not a recipe you can throw some more sugar into. I don't want to be calm. I want to be angry. Henry is dead, Nadia is fighting for her life, and we're still no closer to figuring it out. *Any* of it. This isn't something that can be fixed by sitting around with a cup of tea and a notepad. I might have lost *everything*."

"It may not seem like it right now, but it's not all you—"

"You know what, I think I'm going to brave the rain." Sue ripped off her apron and stormed to the beads, head down. "I'm sorry, Julia. I just ... I need some space. I hope you get everything finished for tomorrow, and I'll see you at the f-funeral tomorrow."

Sue headed off into the rain, and Julia ignored every instinct to call after her, to stop her and bring her back. For once, Julia didn't know how her sister would react. Thunder rumbled, and Julia slammed the door and let out a roar of frustration along with it. The slam echoed around the empty café – a sound she'd heard many times, yet never caused.

Slumping into a chair, Julia pondered how she could stop her sister from sinking further into the quicksand. Sue seemed intent on diving in headfirst, too certain she was going in the right direction to see Julia's hands reaching out.

Maybe that's the problem.

Sue had made it clear.

Stop trying.

"Julia?" Sue's voice reached Julia even before the door hit the bell to announce her abrupt arrival. "Julia, I'm so sorry. I—"

Julia didn't care. She grabbed her sister, already

soaked to the bone. Julia didn't care about that, either. She had no idea how to dance with her sister in her current situation – she'd changed, there was no denying it – but nothing could break their bond. Not all the slammed doors in the world.

Come rain or shine. Even thunder and lightning couldn't stand between them.

"She's awake, Julia," Sue said as she pulled away, wiping her nose with the back of her hand. Red-rimmed eyes stared at her, lifted by a smile so warm Julia forgot she was shivering from her damp clothes. "I got a call when I was running past The Plough. Nadia is awake. She'll know who stabbed her. This could all end tonight."

In fair Verona, where we lay our scene, From ancient grudge break to new mutiny, Where civil blood makes civil hands unclean ... Doth with their death bury their parents' strife ...

Jessie was dreaming.

She had to be.

Looking around the stone courtyard, she could hardly believe she had Shakespeare quotes fixed in her brain. It was such a nice day, too. So warm. Suffocatingly warm. And that bird's chirping had an unnatural, steady rhythm more unsettling than calming.

Nothing felt natural in fair Verona. As though she'd summoned them, people rushed about her from every which way, spinning her like a penny on marble, yet she couldn't feel their touch or her shoes fighting the stone.

She had no time to wonder if she even had feet.

They would pull her into their tide, drag her into their maddening dash around the courtyard like pinballs in a machine. Somehow, she held firm, and as though rewarding her, the crowd parted, and a familiar face walked towards her.

She mirrored that smile of his.

There you are.

Billy, with that stupid smile she hadn't seen in so long, was dressed like he was headed to a fancy dress party at The Globe. He reflected her smile as he marched at her, each stride longer than the last. But despite the smile, his dark eyes glared at her beneath his eyebrows, and her smile dropped. He hated her, she could feel it, and in his grip was something gold.

O happy dagger!

Though Billy was inches from her face, she couldn't make out his features, like she couldn't remember ever looking at them properly. But why was she wasting her thoughts, her time? The blade must have sunk in, yet still, she couldn't help but lunge forward—

—To wake in the chair, gasping as she sucked up the drool that had leaked from the side of her mouth.

Jessie opened her eyes. She still sat in the corner of Nadia's hospital room, but the icky emotions from her subconscious lingered like damp after rain. Maybe Alfie had been right about listening to all those lucid dreaming meditations on plane journeys not being the best idea.

"What's going on?"

The doctors and nurses crowding Nadia's bed didn't acknowledge her. The machines that had lulled her to sleep were still chirping like robotic birds, their rhythm slower than when she'd given in to the fluttering of her eyelids.

Jessie rubbed the sleep from her eyes as she pushed herself out of the chair. She cleared her throat and, catching the eye of a nurse, asked, "What's happening? Is Nadia all right?"

"Are you family? If you're not family, you can't be in here."

Jessie let herself be brushed towards the door, backpack in hand, as she looked back at Nadia. Fair enough. The police who'd been keeping watch outside hadn't noticed her slip in, and now they'd seemed to have given up on their watch altogether.

Through the bodies surrounding the bed, she saw Nadia illuminated by tiny waving torches. She resisted their tugs at her eyelids, thrashing her head on the pillow as she stared up at them with all the expected shock. Jessie had fallen asleep, hoping she'd wake to see Nadia looking back at her.

Not quite, but close enough.

After filling up on a protein bar and a bottle of water from a vending machine, Jessie retraced her footsteps to the corridor where she'd first bumped into Sue. She was glad to see Jenny behind the same desk, minus the chocolates.

Jenny, on the other hand, pretended she didn't notice Jessie when her head whipped back for a second look. "He wasn't a psycho serial killer, you know. Paul the porter. He was actually really sweet."

"I never said he *was* a killer," Jessie replied apologetically. "It's good to check those things, though. Did you have fun?"

Glancing from the screen to Jessie as her fingers worked the keyboard, Jenny pursed her lips and gave an excited little nod. "Took me quad biking. Wasn't really my thing, but I got into it." She accepted a folder from a passing nurse, wheeling her chair to the other side of the desk. "Did you want something? If you're looking for Sue, she's not here."

"I was looking for you, actually," Jessie said,

knowing this was her chance to shoot her shot. She lifted the badge and Jenny glanced at it without really looking. "Auntie Sue might have mentioned that I work for *The Peridale Post*? I'm gathering information to see if all these recent attacks are connected somehow."

"Connected?" Jenny glanced up, even as her pen continued filling in the boxes of the form. "Is this about Dr Khan maybe being the one who stabbed Nadia? I always knew there was something fishy about him, but I could never put my finger on it. Nadia never talked about him, which is a red flag, if you ask me."

"So, you never saw anything? Overheard anything?"

"No," Jenny said, scooping up the phone as she peeped up and down the busy corridor, "but I know someone who did." Her face lit up at the sound of a loud woman on the other end. "Cassandra, grab Matt and get down here. No, you come to me. Because I said so. Because you two need to get up and stretch your legs instead of sitting there gossiping, that's why." She hung up. "They're on their way."

In her post-nap haze, Jessie barely had time to gather what she wanted to ask before the two nurses she recognised from her previous visit snuck around the corner like naughty schoolchildren roaming the halls.

"Where's the fire?"

"Tell this reporter here what you saw the other day, Cassandra," Jenny said, leaning back in her chair with a pleased look. "Don't worry, she's Sue's niece. She's legit."

That easy.

"I feel terrible about it," Cassandra whispered, "but I saw them going into a cubicle. I thought they were having a cheeky little snog, knowing they're married, but … they weren't. He was threatening her. If I'd have said something, if I'd—"

"You thought what anyone else would have," Jessie stated, not wanting to turn over old ground. "We're aware of that particular incident. Is there anything else you might have seen? Anything Nadia might have said?"

"Could barely get two words out of her most days," Matt said, leaning in with a loaded smile. "But I do know something, actually. Is this going to be in the paper?"

"Possibly," Jessie said, showing her badge again. "Probably."

"Will there be pictures?"

Jessie wasn't sure how to answer, but Matt looked excited. Leaning on the corner of the desk, she tilted her ear to him and gave him an encouraging nod. "What do you know?"

Carrot Cake and Concern

"It was New Year's Eve," Matt started in a low voice, leaning so close that Jessie could smell his peppermint chewing gum, "and I was on the dreaded midnight shift."

"We *all* were," Cassandra said, rolling her hands and giving him a tap on the arm. "And don't go around the houses like you usually do. We don't have all day."

"All right, Cassandra," he snapped back, "if you'll *let* me speak." He sighed, and after shooting daggers her way, returned his minty breath to Jessie's ear. "So, New Year's Eve, and I was a total sourpuss because I didn't have a date for the countdown. I went up to the roof because I felt like being dramatic, and fireworks were going off, and well, it just felt like the right time."

"Weren't going to jump off, were you?" Cassandra asked with a hearty laugh. "Get to the point, Matt. Crikey."

"If you interrupt me *one* more time." He took a calming breath. "So, there I am, texting my ex, making the first bad decision of the year in its first minute because why change now?" He pointed a finger up at the ceiling tiles. "But then, a voice from on high told me that I *shouldn't* text my ex. I'd probably had a few too many glasses of champers by that point. I was trying to feel festive and, quite frankly, work or not, I think I deserved it. I'm entitled to – anyway, this voice from upstairs came in a little delayed, so the text had already gone. I threw my phone off the roof and vowed to start my life anew, but I look down and—"

"Did your phone take as long to hit the ground as this story's taking to get to the point?" Cassandra asked flatly.

"There was Dr Khan," he said, steamrolling through. "Marching away from the place. Fuming. *Raging*."

"How could you tell from up there?" Jenny asked. "It's well high up, and it was dark."

"Because he was walking right by the place where the porters have their ciggies when they're not supposed to, on that corner by the morgue, and Dr Khan, as bold as day, walked right up to this poor chap who was just there smoking, and he..." Matt's voice drifted off, his gaze shifting beyond Jessie. He righted himself and held his hand up as two security guards looked around. "If you're looking for that homeless fella who's been sleeping in the dungeons, it's that way and to the left."

They nodded their thanks and went on.

"Fresh and juicy gossip, by the way," he whispered back to excitement. "One of the porters reported that he found someone sleeping down there not thirty minutes ago."

"What did Dr Khan do?" Jessie prompted.

"Oh, he punched the porter square in the face and

threw him down that little hill. I heard Khan had been punched by some greasy-looking bloke earlier that night, and that Nadia was spotted locking tongues with him later on. But like I always say, we've all got a lot going on all the time, and I know that hill is only an incline, but it was as uncalled for as me texting my ex."

"What did you do next?" Jessie asked.

"I went down to see if they were okay, obviously. I found my phone, and I had a text from my ex telling me never to connect him again, which was fair enough. The poor bloke who'd got punched ended up being Paul the porter, so I helped him up, and well, Paul's always game, so I got my New Year's kiss in the end."

"You kissed Paul the porter?" Jenny cried, dragging herself back in. "I *just* went on a date with him."

"Quad biking?" Matt retorted with a devilish smile. "You're welcome to him, Jennifer. I was at a low point, and he had a pulse. You know he lives in a clapped-out caravan in a smelly field, and I'm as much for the tiny living movement as anyone, but there's a difference between..."

Leaving them to their bickering, Jessie trotted down the hall to the left. She had another account of Dr Khan lashing out at someone, and Nadia was awake, but the person sleeping in 'the dungeons' was a new variable she wanted to get to the bottom of.

Her gut had got her this far, and it was on a roll.

Jessie followed the instructions and came to a door labelled MORGUE. If anywhere was a dungeon, it would be this place. She pushed gently on the doors as they burst open from the inside. The force threw her down against the cold rubber floor, rolling her onto her side with a groan. Meaty fingers tightened around her arm and yanked her to her feet before she could process how to get up with dignity. The security guard gave her a scan before sprinting down the corridor, the second thick-necked guard hot on his heels. Somewhere around the corner and further down the ward, metal trays bounced against the same floor Jessie had just slapped. Judging by the vending machine from which she'd just bought a protein bar, she knew where the mystery man was heading, and she knew he wasn't homeless. Far from it.

The soles of Jessie's shoes let out an ear-splitting squeak as she bounded to a halt outside Nadia's room. The man who'd pushed her down was there, dressed from head to toe in tatty black clothes. Jessie didn't blame whoever'd seen him for thinking he was homeless; Dr Khan would easily have blended in on the streets she'd once slept on.

Her feet had set off sprinting while her mind

expected the worst: to walk in on Dr Khan trying to finish what he'd started.

The reality was far different.

Adnan Khan had fallen to his knees at the foot of the bed. The guards caught up and grabbed either side of him, dragging his hands from their clasped begging.

"Tell them, Nadia!" he cried. "Tell them it wasn't me! Please, Nadia. Please. Tell them I didn't stab you. Please. Nadia. *Nadia!*"

Nadia's head rolled on the pillow, turning away, and she closed her eyes. Dr Khan continued to scream, but she acted as though she couldn't hear a thing while the rest of the hospital hushed around him. Jessie tossed the guards her lanyard to tie up his wrists, pocketing the ID badge that had been attached to it.

She'd arrived at the hospital expecting to nail down Dr Khan, and by chance, she'd been there to witness ... she wasn't sure what.

She'd been so convinced Dr Khan was their man, and yet the Dr Khan in her mind, the simmering pot with the fierce growl, hadn't shown up. She looked at Nadia again as her husband's screams faded away, but the woman didn't open her eyes.

"Nadia?" one doctor prompted anyway. "The

police will want to know. Did you see who did this to you? Was it him? Was it Dr Khan?"

Softly, very softly, she said, "I ... I don't remember."

Barker ripped the sheet of paper out of the typewriter, crumpled it, and bounced it into the pile in the corner of the shed as the softening rain pattered above.

What am I trying to prove?

That I can do something?

Anything?

He wound in a fresh sheet, DI Moyes' words still spinning in his ears.

If you wanted to be a detective so much, you shouldn't have thrown your job away.

Barker bashed his fingers down on the keys, trying to return his mind to the time capsule case. Since he'd thought of the title, dozens of opening lines had come to him in showers over the months.

The Body in the Time Capsule.

The perfect follow-up to *The Body in the Basement*, a book he'd given up hope of ever following up. In the shed, he gave up again and ripped out the sheet, resisting the urge to curl up his fists and smash the antique keys into smithereens.

Maybe he wasn't a writer any more than he'd been

a detective inspector. He'd been a decent DI, but the men in suits – the ones Moyes had said wanted him back – had sucked any joy from his career that he might once have had.

Then again, perhaps that had only been another of her flattery techniques.

He'd had a similar struggle with the publishers, too. They'd meddled so much that they'd killed his passion for writing, and now he had a pile of crumpled evidence in the corner to prove they might just have killed it forever.

And it wasn't like the PI cases were coming through.

Any kudos from detective-turned-writer-turned-PI had worn off, leaving him facing the reality that he'd signed up for yet another desk job with suits just as demanding. Only now, he was stalking their spouses and being asked to chase stroke-causing aliens.

Barker jumped as the door blew open, but the wind wasn't the culprit. Jessie was the storm that crashed into the shed. Jessie slammed the door behind her. Soaked from head to toe, she doubled over and let out a scream that would have had the vegetables dropping from their stalks, if there were any to drop.

"I'm sorry," she said, exhaling as her face

unclenched. "I think I was holding that in the whole drive over here."

"If you don't want to scream every so often, are you even living?" Barker kicked the papers under the shelf before giving Jessie a quick hug, but she hadn't let out all her frustration with the scream. She was practically fizzing, and she sprang free to pace. If DI Moyes had been running on fumes, Jessie was fired up on something altogether more potent. "What's going on? Shakespeare got you in a tizzy?"

"Always. But not this time. This isn't Romeo and Juliet. Nadia's awake, and they've arrested Dr Khan."

Barker wanted to let out a sigh of relief that he didn't have to deal with the lingering guilt that came from unsolved cases; he hadn't realised he'd given up halfway through his latest theory, until he hopped over to the typewriter instead. Jessie continued to pace, and the relief didn't come.

"I think I got it all wrong, Barker," she said. "I *know* it. It doesn't feel right. I still think Dr Khan is probably a total toerag, but ... I don't think he stabbed Nadia."

"Didn't she—"

"Memory problems," Jessie cut in, half rolling her eyes. "They said she could remember any time, but it's not unusual for the events surrounding trauma like that to be as scrambled as her guts after that knife got through with them." Jessie paused, still pacing. "But it was Phil who *really* got his guts twisted up. He..." Her voice trailed off, and she glanced at Barker, whose mouth was suddenly dry. "Sorry, poor choice of words. But that's what happened to him. Nadia got one, he got a dozen, and Henry got pills. Surely if the same person attacked them all, the method would have been the same?"

"You'd think so, but each of those murders could have been a spur-of-the-moment decision using whatever was at hand."

"Okay, so someone with a packet of prescription-only pain pills lying around. We already know about Coral, but the rest? A bunch of doctors and nurses wouldn't struggle to get their hands on something strong. How did they get Henry to take them?"

"I'm not sure, but are you sure Dr Khan isn't—"

Jessie clenched her eyes like she wanted to stop any more doubt from clouding her vision. "One stab versus twelve, Barker. Let's say Nadia was killed because she figured it out. Nadia confronted Henry's murderer while everyone else was at the meeting at Sue's place. They grabbed a knife and stabbed her once. Phil was next door, cutting the bushes. Having seen the whole thing, he ran off to tell someone. The lunatic with the knife followed, and stab, stab, stab."

"That's how it seems."

Jessie stopped pacing and stared at him as if she

could see the mental image still burning in his mind's eye. "It's brutal. They must have really *hated* Phil Henderson to do that. But Dr Khan doesn't have any connection to Phil that we know of. If he'd wanted to kill his wife, it would have been out of anger. So ... one stab? If you were really furious and you really wanted to ensure someone would die, you'd ... well. You'd make sure, wouldn't you?"

Jessie was right. Barker had been to his fair share of crime scenes involving knives, and people rarely had just the one wound when someone with a knife in their hand intended to kill. Add in passion? Anger? One wound wouldn't have been enough to satisfy.

"I had an idea earlier," he said, looking out to the empty patch as rain flooded the soil. "I'd been assuming the botched burial came down to whoever was holding the shovel being disturbed and running off. But what if ... what if they were too *upset* to finish what they'd started?"

"Oh?" Jessie stared at him, but the spark flashed as he expected. "*Oh.* You mean ... if the person murdered Phil Henderson like they did because they hated him and only partially buried Henry because they cared too much about him, you're saying Nadia survived because they wanted her to live?"

"Or they didn't *want* to stab her but they still needed her to die."

Barker waited for Jessie to start picking holes in his theory, but she only nodded as she let the details soak in. "So, we're looking for someone who hates Phil Henderson but likes the other two. Not enough to *not* kill them, but enough to not do the world's most precise job."

"That sums it up."

"Then we need to get to your office and finish with those sticky notes," Jessie said, patting him on the shoulder before yanking open the door. A brow drifted up with her smile. "The way I see it, Barker, that narrows it down to just three people."

Only three?

"Oh?" Barker considered who might fit Jessie's description, and his eyes widened as the names of three women came to him. "*Oh.*"

"Oh, indeed."

"Then you might want to hear where my mind was going earlier," Barker said as he followed her out into the rain, looking down at his pricked finger, "because there's a certain woman – let's say she lives in a forest and loves lying – who ticks all those boxes, and then some."

14

"hat do you think, Sue?"

"Sorry?"

"About the prescription pills?"

Despite the rush of questions swirling through Julia's mind, she placed the notepad atop the stack of cakes in plastic boxes, all ready to go to Sharon's for Henry's funeral. With no idea how many people she was supposed to be preparing for, Julia had kept baking late into the night, while Barker and Jessie hashed out the details of the case in the basement office. Having heard Jessie's theory before they shut themselves downstairs, Julia had written a similar list of notes while waiting for oven space.

"I'm sorry," Sue said, tugging down the hem of her

black, high-necked dress after wriggling off the stool. "I'm a little distracted today. Yes, there's probably a way to prove if Coral was handed her prescription. If she collected it at the hospital or a chemist, there will have been cameras. It won't be easy, though. We're talking about a knee surgery that happened months ago. Do you really think she could have killed her son?"

As a parent, Julia quelled her instincts to deny the possibility. "Barker wants us to keep an open mind. She's one of the options."

"And the others?"

"Sharon and Abbie."

"Oh, right." Sue looked relieved; had she thought Julia suspected her? "I could ask around at the hospital about Coral, if they ever let me back in."

Do you want to go back? was what Julia wanted to ask, but she wouldn't go further. Not today. Sue seemed to have expelled her rage with the thunder, but she was no less upset now that patches of blue shone through wispy clouds.

"Sharon left the meeting early," Sue pointed out, something Julia had underlined in her notes. "Nadia was stabbed around that same time. Abbie was also in the area, and they were both at the launch party two weeks ago. I spoke with Nadia this morning."

"How is she?"

"Recovering. Still doesn't remember what happened, and she said Adnan's taken a vow of silence on the advice of his lawyer."

"Does she think it could have been him?"

"I don't think she knows what to think, and it's probably best not to force the memories. They'll spring free of their own accord when she's ready. She's almost certain that Sharon's the mole who sold us out. She was so against our demonstration."

"Do you think she'd turn on you like that?"

"Think about it," Sue said with a shrug. "She was trying to get her daughter into a meeting on the chance she might want to go into nursing one day. Jenny noticed the pattern. She only tried to get Abbie in on days she had to rush off, and Abbie never seemed that bothered." The thin strap of Sue's handbag went over her exposed shoulder, and she slipped into the shoes waiting under the island. "I need to get to the service."

"Will you be okay?"

Sue thought about her answer and lowered her head before shaking it. Looking up with a smile, she said, "I lied to you about knowing Henry well. When you first brought him up, I panicked and played dumb. Last thing I wanted was to end up in that little pad of yours. The truth is, I got to know each Henry really well, actually. And no, I can see that look in your eyes. It wasn't like *that*. That's why I didn't tell you. It was strictly platonic."

"Like me and Johnny?"

"Exactly, except Henry never fancied me. He only had eyes for Nadia. I know I only knew the man for four months, but he really changed me." Parting the beads, she paused and looked back, her head bowed. "You think I've been bad these last few weeks? You should have seen me when I actually gave up. Henry inspired me back to life that New Year's Eve, and I'm absolutely heartbroken that he's dead. I can't believe I tried to act any different." She looked like she was on the verge of tears, but she sniffed them back. "I'm sorry I can't help you get all of this over there."

Julia stomped the signal to Barker on the floor. "It's fine. We've got it covered."

Sue left through the empty café, and Julia glanced at the clock. Melissa was ten minutes late for what should have been her third day, and she had one minute to keep up the only tradition she'd managed to make. Julia pulled out her phone and scanned the island filled with stacked cake boxes. She really hoped there'd be enough.

"Hickory dickory dock, the mouse ran down the

clock," Jessie cried, kicking open the back door. She'd changed into her suit and had on shades Julia was sure belonged to Sue. "It's ten past eight, Melissa's late, and Julia's probably watching the clock."

Her phone lit up right on time.

One new text from Melissa: *Sick.*

"We're down to a single word," Jessie said, snatching up the phone. She typed in Julia's passcode before her thumbs fired out a message. "It's for your own good, Mum, so don't try to stop me. We need to focus today."

Jessie had sent a text message before Julia could take her device back. Jessie had said everything Julia really wanted to say about professionalism and making good first impressions, but she'd done it without it taking hours of googling and texting back and forth with Roxy and Johnny to confirm the wording.

"'Due to your current lack of availability,'" Julia read aloud as Dot and Barker joined them, "'it is with regret that your trial at Julia's Café has been cancelled. I hope you get well soon, and I wish you luck with your job search.'"

"Another one bites the dust?" Dot adjusted her black tie. "Here, Julia, settle this for us. *I* think we look like *The Blues Brothers*, but Barker and Jessie think we look like *Men in Black*, which is in quite poor taste considering what happened to Mrs Hardy's—"

"'You still paying me?'" Julia interrupted Dot as the next message came in fresh. "What do I say?"

"*No*," came the reply from three directions.

Julia sent the one-word message and instantly received an emoji of a hand gesture that might have gained her a broken finger and a trip to A&E if she'd offered the same to Dot. Julia blocked Melissa's number, deleted the conversation, and let out a sigh of relief.

"Like I said," Jessie announced, pushing her glasses into her hair before squatting to hug a stack of cakes against the front of the suit she'd found in the charity shop, "you need to stop falling for them in the interviews."

"Are you sure you want to stay closed today, Julia?" Dot asked, picking up a tray of buffet food in each hand. "Percy said he'd watch the place."

Julia patted the pocket of the black jacket she'd borrowed from Sue. "We've been paid more than enough upfront, and we should probably—"

"Let's *go*, alien hunters!" Jessie cried from the back gate, and the glasses fell back onto her nose with a bob of her head. "Our suits are fresh, and the sun is shining. I'd say it's the perfect day to put this case to bed so Henry Foreman can actually rest in peace."

Carrot Cake and Concern

Scooping up her column of cake boxes, Julia wanted nothing more. She thought of little else as she drove her packed car to the gates of Henderson Place. The fleet was led by Julia, with the Mini in the middle, and Barker trailing at the back. For whatever reason, he'd insisted Dot be his passenger.

Julia was grateful if it was because he was giving her some silence to stew.

And stew she did.

About Abbie, the elusive not-really-related-niece of Henry, who'd been so infatuated she'd crashed a New Year's Eve party to declare her love. And she might have been in on her not-really-her-mother's role as the mole in the group.

Sharon was the odd one out, and she'd only gained access to the group thanks to Henry's advocacy. Now, the person Henry had loved had changed her mind about her deciding vote.

Julia could only think of one reason the most precise surgeon around didn't want to rock the boat. Deep behind her gates, she lived the most comfortable life for miles around.

Julia drove through the second set of gates, and the houses she'd been waiting to see finally came into view. Slowing down, she ducked to take in the arched row of giant houses. As big as the mansions were, they were situated just as far apart. They might very well have been the most unusual collection of houses Julia had ever seen, but they were still more impressive than anything a Wellington could have built in the 1800s.

At first glance, the houses were built primarily from glass. As she crawled along the butter-smooth road, stone columns and wooden beams jumped out. Natural as the elements were, they looked like they'd been added in a feeble attempt to blend the structures into the nature they'd trampled all over. No amount of texture could disguise that the houses looked like they had arrived from another planet.

Julia had no idea what they were doing in the Cotswolds.

Maybe it wasn't such a bad idea that they were hidden behind the wall.

Sharon was waiting on her doorstep, illuminated by a glowing chandelier of spiralling copper glass in the cavernous entrance hall behind her. She wore a black dress, a pair of heels that made Julia's ankles hurt to look at, and a sour expression. Julia glanced at the clock; she was ten minutes late.

Fair enough, she thought, though she blamed the driveway. They must have milk helicoptered in when they ran out, or maybe they had cows hidden in the trees that had survived Henderson's flattening. Perhaps there were even rows of shops she didn't know about; the place was bigger than the village she called home.

"Inside," Sharon said, skipping the berating as Julia climbed out of her car. Her glare went to the stack of cake boxes secured by the seatbelt in the front of her vintage car. In this insanely rich place behind the walls, the poor Anglia looked like a tin can that had blown out of the recycling bin. "Is that all you've made? I knew I was taking a risk hiring a small business. I thought the deposit would be enough to..."

Sharon's voice trailed off as Jessie and Barker rounded the trees. Julia had been too in awe to glance in her rear-view mirror to check they were following behind. The sea of boxes summoned a calmer breath from Sharon, though her statuesque posture never seemed to soften.

"Right, well, it seems you've made use of the deposit I gave you," she said, unclipping her bag. She tossed another envelope of money onto the stack of cakes as Julia tiptoed up glass steps to the front doors. "You'll get the rest at the end."

Julia resisted the urge to say *the rest?* as she stared at what had to be another thousand pounds in colourful cash. Sharon whisked off, leaving Julia to try to keep her mouth from gaping open as she walked into an entrance hall shimmering like the inside of a glass paperweight.

"How much does she think the price of food has gone up?" Jessie whispered as she followed Julia into a grand green-marble kitchen tucked away at the back of the house.

A garden stretched out as long as the road from Sue's house to the gates. Julia could just about make out the red wall through the trees – the same red wall they'd built right up to the edge of a local beauty spot. The neighbours at Number Two were so far away, Julia couldn't see into their garden, but she imagined it was also a football field of grass cut in perfect lines, like Sharon's.

They were the most perfect lines she'd ever seen, and the house was artistic and chic, yet the whole place left her feeling cold. The waste of space was enormous, and it made Julia wish she'd ventured down to the vale and the forest more frequently before it was reduced to this.

Like Henry and Phil, no amount of regret would bring the vale back. Julia cracked open the first lid and started arranging the buffet.

"You're not going to believe this," Barker said as he carried in another stack of boxes. "Looks like we're not the only fleet being let into this place today."

"The hippies are here!" Dot cried as she bustled around him with a tray of sandwiches balancing on each flat palm. "Julia, how long did it take you to make all of this?"

"Most of yesterday, some of this morning."

"By the looks of what's coming, I think you might have needed an extra week."

15

Jessie leaned over the edge of the balcony as Sharon diverted the last of the stragglers to the door, shouting after them to "Keep moving straight to the gate."

Given how confused Sharon had been when people started turning up to celebrate the life of her brother, Jessie was surprised she'd let the hundreds of people stay as late as sunset. Jessie snapped one last picture, though her phone was already bursting with plenty. She'd vowed to grab a quote from every person who walked through the doors, but they'd kept turning up. If she had, Johnny's final issue would have comprised hundreds of quotes about Henry, which certainly would have made up for his past press appearances, at least.

In all the quotes, the sentiment was clear. The people who'd shown up to say goodbye to Henry had been touched or inspired by him in some way. They painted a picture of a soldier never scared to back down from a battle.

A man who cared about peace and justice.

A man who deserved more than to end up with the carrots.

Jessie noticed her mum in the kitchen, but Julia had long-since stopped keeping an eye on her. She'd been deep in her thoughts whenever Jessie, hunting for Abbie, had passed her. The daughter hadn't been among the funeral party, though Jessie eventually found her on her third 'where's the bathroom' wander of the glass maze.

"Abbie, isn't it?" Jessie walked straight into the room without knocking. "Can I ask you some questions about Henry Foreman?"

Glaring at Jessie from her bed, Abbie dragged down her headphones, and cried, "You shouldn't be in here!"

"I'm not a guest, I've been working."

"I can see that, and you still shouldn't be in here." Abbie looked around as though deciding if she should call out. "What do you want?"

Jessie knew she'd have one shot at getting what she needed from Abbie, and that the ID badge in her pocket wouldn't make a difference to the teenager.

"Do you like your stepmum?"

"Can't stand her," she replied bluntly as heavy metal blasted from the headphones around her neck. "Waiting for the fat check Phil left me in his will to hit my account, and then I'm gone like Donkey Kong. Sharon's a total psycho."

"Do you think she killed Henry?"

Abbie shrugged, and Jessie noticed a hint of sadness in her eyes. Jessie'd only found Abbie because the girl had been peering at the party over the balcony like a guest who hadn't been invited.

"Dunno, but she can rot with Phil, for all I care. She thinks I can't tell, but she's been trying to get me to say I'll put her in my will now that she knows I'll be loaded. Here, you can give her this if she's sent you in to spy on me." Abbie snatched open her bedside drawer and tossed a burgundy ring box across her white carpet. "Tell her she knows I took it. Don't even know why she wants it anyway. It's ugly."

Jessie bent down and picked up the box. A diamond bigger than any she'd ever seen sat on a silver band buried in the box. From the slight tarnish, she could tell it was older than the two of them combined, but it still sparkled like it had been freshly polished.

"You stole Coral's ring?"

"Sharon said it was *her* ring." She went to put her headphones back up, and with a curl in her lip, asked, "Anything else?"

Jessie considered asking Abbie about her crush on Henry, but to call it a romance would have had Shakespeare rolling in his grave. She could see why Henry hadn't given in to her New Year's Eve tantrum. From the people she'd interviewed, he hadn't been much into romance anyway.

Nadia was his exception.

"What will you do with the money?" Jessie asked.

"Might go to LA and start my rap career. Or maybe I'll just disappear into the woods and become like … an artist, or something. Dunno. Anywhere but Henderson Place. Why? You're not about to start begging for cash, are you? Because if you are…"

"Coral, wait!" Barker called, wedging his foot in the door before she crammed it shut. "This is the last time, I promise."

"You said that when I came to your office, Mr Brown. I've been most obliging with you. Now I asks that you leave me alone for real. I'm entitled to my privacy."

"I know you lied about knowing who took your ring. I know you spoke with someone behind my allotment."

"I don't know what you're talking about, Mr—"

"Was it Abbie?" Barker said. Coral stopped slamming the door on his foot. "Did you not want to tell the police because she's a kid?"

"I don't tells the police anything I don't needs to," she said, glaring at him with those big green eyes. "How is it you know it was her for certain?"

Barker reached into his pocket and pulled out the box Jessie had handed to him. Coral's face lit up, and the door shut, reopening moments later, minus the chain. He popped open the box, and she lunged, but he snapped it back.

"That's mine," Coral said, grabbing Barker by the ear and yanking him down, twisting until he relinquished it. "How dare you tease me with *my* family heirloom?"

"But you admit that Abbie stole it?"

Coral's throat revved like an engine as she stroked the diamond, staring up at Barker. "All right, I admits it. Yeah, someone saw her sniffing around my cottage, and I realised it was around the time I last saw the ring. I usually keep it locked away, but Henry wanted it to propose to Nadia on New Year's. Told him it was a silly thing to do, what with her being married and all, but he knew she was miserable. He told me he fought with that doctor, and she promised she'd leave with him, but she changed her mind and stayed. Poor Henry still thought he could save her. You know they were in love when they were kids in school?"

"I didn't know that."

"Her dad kept 'em apart. Poor mites. If they'd married as they should have, my Henry might still be alive."

Coral snapped the box shut and dabbed at her nose before dropping the ring into her cardigan pocket. Something rattled inside, and Barker remembered seeing her shove something into the same cardigan on his last visit.

"The pills," he said, holding the door before she could close it. "I know you had a prescription for the same pills that killed Henry. You can try and deny it, Coral, but I need you not to. Someone's claiming you're a liar."

"I'm *no* such thing!"

"You lied to me."

"I don't trust you, so I don't owes you the truth, Mr Brown." Coral's hand went to the cardigan, pulling out the pills. "For indigestion, Mr Brown. I swear on Henry's life I was never given any painkillers after my op, and I wouldn't have taken 'em if they had."

"But I know you're—"

Coral reached up and grabbed his ear again, twisting it even harder. "Call me a liar again, Mr Brown, and I'll make sure you regret it. I never had any pills."

Barker reached into his pocket and pulled out the picture he'd run back to his office to grab. Wincing through the pain, he turned it the right way up.

"That's my mum," he said. Coral let go of him to take the picture. "It's coming up on ten years since she passed, and, laying my cards on the table, I miss her. You remind me of her. It's silly, I know. Means nothing, but it's just an energy thing. I *want* to believe you're telling the truth, but someone has accused you of not just lying about pills and rings, but about your life. Where did you live before your husband died?"

"First of all, I was never married, and second, I've *always* lived here. I already tolds you. Generations of my family have passed this house and this ring down. Why would I lie about that?"

"I – I'm not sure."

"Here." She thrust the picture back at Barker and marched into the house. He wasn't sure he was invited in, but he followed. The old dog glanced up at him, blinked, and returned to the fire. "You're not the only one with photographs."

Coral dumped a mountain of pictures on the dining table and spread them about with her hands.

Barker wasn't sure how she knew what she was looking for, but she plucked one out.

"That's my mum sat in *that* chair over there with me as a little girl," she said, pulling out another. "Great Aunt's wedding in the forest just over there. Garden was bigger back then. This is my great-great-grandmother, who passed down the ring. According to my mum, she was a maid at Wellington Manor. She was either a secret mistress or she stole the ring, but it's worth a few bob, and my family have always saved it for the next generation, just in case."

Barker rummaged through the photographs, from glossy colour snaps all the way back to black and white portraits with white frilly edges. The history of an entire family crammed in a shortbread biscuit tin. The cottage tied them all together, and though Coral could have acquired the pictures from someone else, he believed her.

He always had. But he'd had to be sure.

"My next question is," Barker said, taking a deep breath as he pocketed the photograph of his mum, "if your daughter doesn't need the money and clearly doesn't care much about your family, why did she send her stepdaughter here to steal your only family heirloom? And more importantly, do you think that's the reason your daughter murdered your son?"

16

"Julia, it's all in there," Sue whispered, handing the paper folder through the crack in the glass door at Number One, Henderson Place. "I asked around to see if Sharon was in the operating theatre like she told you. Not only is there *no* record of her clocking in at the hospital, but the private parking space that Phil bought for her, which she goes *ballistic* if anyone parks in, was empty all day. Sharon left our meeting early and didn't go to the hospital. I think she came here."

"I think you're right," Julia whispered, looking back at the dim house of glass; the thing creaked when nobody was around. "I haven't been able to stop thinking about it. It just makes sense. The one stab, the twelve stabs, the pills."

"There's something else, too, but I can't stay. They're holding the gates open for me, so I need to be quick. You're going to give it to the police, aren't you?"

"Absolutely." Julia pushed forward her brightest smile as she tucked the folder under her arm, like she wasn't even going to look at it. "I'm just waiting for Jessie and Barker to finish up, then I'll be heading home."

"Give Olivia a cuddle for me."

Julia promised she would and closed the door. It would be the perfect way to end the day. A cuddle with Olivia and a solved case. She cracked open the folder Sue had passed her and set off up the stairs that swirled around the copper chandelier. She'd seen Jessie tracing the stairs for the first half of the day, but she hadn't seen her for at least an hour. Barker, either, for that matter. She'd been so deep in her own thoughts, she hadn't even cared if people loved the buffet, though the spread had barely lasted fifteen minutes.

Julia walked past the landing Jessie had been preoccupied by. A girl sat on her bed, off in whatever universe her headphones had blasted her to. Looking down at the photographs, Julia carried on up the second staircase; each glass step creaked like a door desperate for oil.

The top pictures in the folder showed an empty

parking space, followed by a blank day on a timesheet. The following two pictures were much more incriminating.

Looking down at the far-off entrance hall, Julia climbed above the chandelier to the very top of the staircase and the archway into which she'd watched Sharon skulk after she'd slammed the door behind the last of Henry's many friends, neglecting to check if anyone was hiding in the bathroom.

"Ssssharon," Julia whispered as she walked into the room. "Are you in here?"

The room was as wide as a bowling alley, with walls of exposed stone boxing in a glass ceiling that stared uninterrupted at the night sky. There was a bed atop a plinth on one side of the long room, and a steaming copper bath on the other. Sharon was perched on the edge of the bath in a black silk robe, angled away from Julia while pouring bath salts into the water. She was sniffling, obviously crying, but even believing she was alone, Sharon didn't give the tears much space.

Even considering what Julia was there to say, the moment felt too intimate for her to witness. She cleared her throat.

"*Excuse* me!" Sharon cried as the tub of bath salts hit the floor and smashed on contact. "Look what you made me do. How dare you come up here to my private quarters. If this concerns the rest of your money, I'm not sure you…"

Julia pulled the most recent envelope Sharon had thrown at her from her jacket pocket and tipped it upside down. The notes fluttered out, soon followed by the contents of the second envelope. Julia shook out both envelopes and tossed out the pictures one by one.

Sharon could see what she was doing, she couldn't look away, but she only stared at Julia. At some point, while Julia had been sprinkling out the contents of the envelopes, Sharon had dipped her fingers into something she was now rubbing into her elbows. Her face had the same shiny sheen to it, too, and she looked tired without her makeup and her sleek waves.

No longer a statue, just a human. Julia felt like she'd entered a place very few had ever seen. Despite what she'd just done, Sharon continued to stare and moisturise, moving up her arms and to her hands.

"This is five hundred pounds a bottle," she said, holding up a tiny jar. "It's made from a very specific jelly from these very rare bees that have a sting so deadly, very few dare reach their hands into their hives. Only a select number of tubs are made a year. People sit three years on waiting lists for one of these tiny pots. Can you believe that?"

"The world can be a baffling place."

Sharon examined the bottle before tossing it across the room. It landed expertly in the bin; Sue had said the woman was precise. "It smells awful and feels like glue. Nothing is ever quite as you think it's going to be. Life? Rather ... *disappointing*."

"Depends how you set yourself up," Julia offered, stepping forward to kick one of the pictures of the empty parking space towards her. "If you build it chasing a lie, then yes, I imagine it can be disappointing. I'm not disappointed. Far from it."

"How excellent for you." Sharon stared down at her, still the little person in her eyes. "How simple a life it must be."

"Simple." Julia agreed with a smile. "The truth is often *quite* simple when you have all the right ingredients. Like, for example, when you told me you were in theatre when Nadia was stabbed. You probably didn't count on that meaning anything to me, but it's something that's so easily checked, and you know my sister works in the hospital. The hospital you went nowhere near that day because you were here all along. Well, a *few* doors down. You've sliced people up your whole career, and I hear you're good at it, but I imagine stabbing someone feels quite different, doesn't it?"

Julia waited for something, but Sharon continued sit on the bath edge and stare, ruffling the water's surface with her fingertips. She pulled her hand out, flicking the droplets all over the pictures.

"Anything else?"

"Your mum's knee," Julia continued. "You operated on it and prescribed her those pills, which, as you can see in these two pictures, you then pocketed."

"I could have given them to her after."

"But you didn't."

"So, I took her pills?" Sharon fanned a fake yawn. "Lock me up. She was never going to take them. She's a simple woman; I know her."

Julia wasn't sure what she'd expected, but watching Sharon casually prepare a bath after throwing away bee venom moisturiser hadn't been it. Julia knew she was right, she just had to figure out a way to crack her.

"Yes, you do," Julia agreed, joining Sharon on the other side of the bath. She ran her hands through the scorching water. "I don't know the truth about how you were raised, but looking at you compared with what I heard about your brother today, it's obvious that you were raised differently, given the outcome. You were the daughter she pushed away, and yet your brother, Henry, she couldn't seem to let go of. Does it hurt that she won't let you in?"

"*I* don't want to let *her* in."

"So, why did you bring her to my café?" Julia

asked, arching a brow. "Why did you offer your home, somewhere locked behind two gates to keep you to yourself, for Henry's friends? You've never stopped wanting her approval, have you, Sharon?"

Sharon was still staring, but the intrigue and amusement had gone. If looks could kill, Julia would have doubled over into the hot water right then.

"The difference between me and Henry is that I applied myself at school," Sharon stated, her spine hardening as she seemed to grow on the other side of the bath. "Not at first, no. Our mother really did want us to stay as *simple* as her. One with nature. No thoughts, empty mind. Just an empty vessel to please others. That's how she likes us. It's why she liked Henry – my poor, sweet, stupid baby brother. Viewed himself as a saviour of man, and yet I couldn't speak with him without falling into the intellectual chasm put between us by his decision to settle exactly where he started."

"Henry helped a lot of people," Julia said, thinking back to Sue's raw emotions that morning in the café. "He inspired people. He cared about things, and—"

"All so he didn't have to get a job." Sharon cackled, suddenly standing. Julia remained seated on the bath's hard edge. "Don't talk like you knew him. He was like a puppy, stumbling around, blind to himself, blind to the reality of the world. He thought his sad, pathetic voice could make a difference in a world like this. Oh, what sweet *delusion* my mother tried to raise us under. What *ignorance* she expected from us, to walk about the world only seeing the good in the little people."

"You save people's lives. What's the difference?"

"I am an *excellent* surgeon," she said. "I've made sure of it. There's no room for anyone to say otherwise. I could have stayed like my mother, living in that cottage forever, rotting, decaying, helpless, with only the system to fall back on. Why would anyone choose that? Henry should have stayed away. He was twenty-seven. It wasn't too late for him. He could have freed himself."

"He left two weeks before his death," Julia said, thinking back to the notepad in her pocket. "And he wasn't seen again, which makes me think he returned on launch night. Did he come back to see you, or was he just unlucky?"

Sharon's lips sprang into a smile that she struggled to hold back.

"I'm sorry. It's just ... maybe I'm not as smart as I think."

"Excuse me?"

"Maybe *I'm* the idiot?" Sharon laughed, shaking her head. The bath was almost full to the brim. "Because how is it, after being so *careful* to cover my tracks, a caveman like him and a ... a ... a *cake woman* noticed what I was up to? It simply makes no sense."

Ah, there she is.

The real Sharon.

The smartest woman to come out of the forest thought she was the smartest woman in the room. Probably any room. Every room. She'd done nothing but flaunt her superiority, but it was as much an act as her perfect posture.

"Cake woman?" Julia replied, twisting the taps to turn off the water. She checked the bath one last time before flicking her fingers in Sharon's direction. "Say I was born a few centuries ago – when things *were* simpler and we still lived in the forests – and if there was somehow sugar, they'd probably have called me that. I love baking the same way you like slicing people up on operating tables. We're good at it. When the walls fall in and the sky goes black, at least we've always got *our* thing, right? The special thing people praise us for. My mum was *really* encouraging with my baking. Those little shreds of positivity meant I could feel good about it. But unlike you, my baking was never about *proving* something. It was about passion. Your brother was passionate about a lot of things. As is your mother. From you, all I seem to understand is that you love ... this?"

Julia gestured to the long, empty room, but Sharon

was back to staring blankly at her. She still hadn't admitted to killing anyone, and Julia had been hoping Jessie or Barker would have come looking for her by now.

"You know what *this* cake woman thinks?" Julia carried on, with one final sigh. "I think you loved your brother in *your* way. I think you wanted him to break free of your mother and find *his* way. I also think you couldn't accept that he chose that life when *you* didn't. Did you think he'd follow you out and you'd have someone on your side in the end? Someone with whom you could stand up to your mother?"

Sharon blinked rapidly, tears forming. She clenched her eyes in defiance, but they rolled down her cheeks.

"I think Henry came back here to ask if you were the mole in FUN. To—"

"He didn't know," Sharon interrupted harshly. "I gave it away by mistake that night. He was here, one last time, to take Nadia away. I knew it was my last chance to stop FUN in their tracks. If I could convince their leader it wasn't a good idea—"

"Why wasn't it a good idea, Sharon?" Coral walked into the bathroom, and Sharon jumped. Julia hadn't heard her creep up the stairs, too entranced by Sharon finally talking. "Your brother was trying to help them nurses, that's all. Were you that scared he'd mess up your life?"

"That hospital was *my* thing," she said. "*Mine.* We were dodging *all* of that. I thought our staff *knew* better. I thought they *cared* more. I thought—"

"You thought you could kill this cause?" Coral roared, and Sharon shrank back. "I've been protesting alongside nurses for years. Before *you* were born. Things repeat around here, like I repeated my parents' mistakes with Henry. I know I held him back, I'm no fool, but you ... I don't know where I went wrong. Why'd you tell Mr Brown all those lies about your childhood?"

"Because that's what I *wanted* to be true when I was little," she growled through gritted teeth. "I used to sit in that crumbling mess of a cottage and dream that I had a different life, once upon a time, so I didn't have to accept that *that* was all I was worth." She tossed her hand in a dismissive gesture. "How did you expect me to go to school with *normal* people without wanting something *more*? Do you remember what I told you when I said I was going to university?"

Coral shrank into herself and didn't say anything.

"Do you?"

Coral shook her head.

"No, I didn't think you would," she said, turning away as she wrapped her arms around herself. "I was thirteen. You told me it would be a waste of time, that I was *wasting my time* trying to make something of myself, and I never would. You didn't want us to do better than you because it would prove you'd done nothing with your life."

"I've done—"

"You've never been farther away than five miles in each direction," Sharon cut her off with a hiss. "You didn't even come to his funeral today. You know he asked for you when I gave him those pills?" She stepped towards her mother, and Coral recoiled, skidding on the money strewn about the floor. "He never could turn down a handout. How was he to know caviar wasn't supposed to taste like *that*? Why would he, when he'd lived off cabbage and carrots his whole sad life."

"You *did* kill him," Coral said, backing away. "And Nadia? You stabbed her too?"

"She figured it out. Always too smart for her own good. Henry told her he was coming to see me, to ask me to take over the group in their absence. She was waiting for him on the back path with her bags."

Julia's heart cracked in two.

"Heartless enough to kill him, knowing that he was about to have his chance at love," Coral said, finding her voice again, "but not so heartless that you could bring yourself to bury him. But what does it matter? You still went on to kill Phil Henderson."

"I thought *you'd* be pleased with that one," Sharon cried. "He saw me stab Nadia through the window. I always said he designed these houses with too much glass. I won't lie. That one felt good. God, I'm so glad I didn't sign a prenuptial agreement. With all the properties he gave me, you'll never have a clue where to even start looking. Don't try to follow me. You know I'll kill you."

Sharon hurried across the bathroom, clutching her silk dressing gown. She paused to slip her feet into heels by the door. After all those stairs, Julia couldn't imagine doing the reverse in heels, but Sharon had proved how much of a statue she was.

If she truly felt anything, Julia wasn't sure.

But she must have felt her ankle twist as she rushed out the door. She turned, reaching out, and caught herself on her other foot. A relieved sigh escaped her as she steadied herself, and after shaking out her foot, she crammed it back into her shoe and set off sprinting, like a surgeon off to theatre.

Except she only managed a few steps before the already twisted ankle buckled again. She staggered to the side, catching herself on the glass banister.

Sharon laughed slowly as she put her weight on it to drag herself up. All her weight. Julia heard the crack before she saw the lines shattering across the thin glass panel, the only barrier between the stairs and the drop.

Sharon froze, but the damage was done. The glass sheet gave way, and she looked back in one last moment of horror.

"I'm sorry," she mouthed.

Julia turned away, but she heard Sharon hit the copper and glass chandelier and then the floor. She let out a sigh and perched on the bath before she could fall to the ground herself.

"No, you're not sorry," Coral said, walking towards the door. She turned around and showed Julia a diamond bigger than any she'd ever seen. "I used to have to pry this ring from her. She'd take it any chance she could get. She'd sit with it on her hand, hidden away in the forest, staring into it for hours and hours, losing herself in it. Losing her mind. Many years ago, I warned my daughter not to live her life to spite me, but I never saw that I was the one who planted the bad seeds."

Coral stared into the ring as she twirled it under the light. She took a few steps onto the glass landing, and Julia crept after her, reaching for her arm and holding her back from making the same mistake as her daughter. Coral tossed the diamond over the edge and said, "You want it? It's yours."

Julia helped Coral down the stairs, passing Abbie, still obliviously listening to her music. Coral couldn't take her eyes off her daughter, but Julia only stole one glance to confirm Sharon was dead – the statue lay broken where hundreds had been standing only an hour ago.

Julia's wished she could have told them all it would be over soon.

Julia couldn't wait to leave Henderson Place, and it sounded like a helicopter had come to pick them up.

Jessie was still catching her breath from sprinting back to her flat to fetch the 3D-printed key from her college bag when the police helicopters landed in the giant gardens behind the glass houses. Barker used the key to open the gates that had been locked on their return, and Julia and Coral walked out of the house arm in arm.

"Coral, how did you get in?" Jessie said, not having noticed when they'd lost track of her following behind on their rush to find Julia. "Is it—"

"Sharon's dead," Coral said, pulling away from Julia to continue hobbling onwards alone. "And there's more than one way into this place, you know.

Now, if you don't mind, I'm going back to my cottage. I think I'd like to never be disturbed again."

The three of them watched Coral make her way down the side of the wall as police cars zoomed up the road behind them the officers who'd opted to fly in. Even surrounded by sirens and whirring blades, Jessie felt at peace there for the first time.

She hadn't been right about Dr Khan, but she trusted Nadia to do the right thing and ditch him. She had a second chance at life. And wherever he'd gone, Henry was free to fight his next fight.

Romeo and Juliet, maybe, but Juliet got to live.

Jessie would take it. She pulled out her phone.

"Hey," Alfie said when he finally picked up. "What's up?"

"Not a lot," she said, glancing at Julia and Barker, talking to DI Moyes by the gates. "Remember that arcade we went to in Japan, where I whooped your behind at *Pac Man*?"

"Vividly."

"Did you let me win?"

"Nope," he said. She believed him. "Jessie, what's up? Are you drunk?"

"On life and Shakespeare only," she said, laughing to herself. She was delirious, she knew it, but she'd just run what had to be a few miles to get a key she hadn't even needed; Julia had got there anyway.

Delirious and brave enough, she said, "Can you text me Stefan's number? We left Berlin quickly and I didn't have a chance to get it."

"Why?" That familiar accusatory tone seeped in. "Are you going to call him?"

"Maybe. Maybe not. Just send me the number, okay? Love you! Gotta go."

Jessie hung up as Johnny rushed at them, camera poised. He'd missed the climax of his final story, but Jessie had a phone full of the newsworthy pictures and quotes they needed to finally let the world know just who Henry Foreman had really been.

"It's totally insane," DI Moyes said, plucking a spring roll from the Chinese takeaway trays in the shed at Barker's allotment later that night. "To think, a deep-seated jealousy of her brother, mixed with not wanting her reputation to be tarnished for being a mole in a group she was trying to bring down from the inside, and just like that, two people are dead. And as usual, your wife beats us all to the punch. You know how cool I thought the helicopters would be?"

"They were cool," Barker assured her, "and don't worry, that's just Julia. You'll get used to her." He dunked a chicken ball in sweet and sour sauce. "This used to be a tradition with Christie. Chinese after a big case to celebrate."

"You miss it?"

"Him?"

"Just that period in your life."

Barker thought about the man he'd spent so much time with since getting the keys to the allotment, and he shook his head. "I think I like exactly where I am right now."

"Does that mean I can tell PC Puglisi he's going to get his new Barker Brown book?" She nodded at the typewriter on the shelf above them. They'd opted to sit on the floor. "He really hasn't been able to stop talking about it."

"Maybe," he replied. "So, does this mean we're friends, then?"

"I thought we already were?"

"The other day—"

"I was a total monster, and I apologise," she said. "You know what it's like. I'd been on my feet all day, and let's just say Coral isn't the only one with sore knees, and shoulders, and hips..." She offered a smile before taking a puff of her electronic cigarette. "Don't worry, it's chronic and I was born with it. Just a silly joint thing."

"That's how you spotted Coral's limp."

"And how I knew the painkiller was the same as

what killed Henry. The first officer who read it didn't recognise that he was seeing a generic and a brand name of the same thing. Finding those pictures of Sharon at the eleventh hour was all I needed, but like I said, too late. Oh, before I forget. I heard this belongs to your wife."

DI Moyes pulled out an envelope filled to the brim with cash. Barker, already knowing Julia would never want to see Sharon's blood-soaked money again, was certain he could find a local nurse's charity that could turn it into something gold.

"So, Laura, why did you move here?" Barker said as he put the money with the spare key. "Have you really fallen in love with Roxy Carter that quickly?"

"Easy, Brown," she said, throwing a spring roll at him. "I never thought I'd have a second chance at love, but the transfers aligned, so I'm seeing where things go."

"You know what, pal," he said, toasting his beer bottle with hers, "I don't think you and me are all that different."

17

By Easter Sunday and the church fete, Peridale had calmed down to its usual spring rhythm. Riverswick's eventful week had barely sewn its seeds in the village, even after Sharon Henderson's confession and death.

Even on Saturday, with only standing room in the café, the conversation was about the weather – though Johnny's final issue had caused a wave on Friday, when Shilpa put them outside the post office next door. Johnny had left off all mention of Riverswick, and Julia and Jessie had enjoyed hearing the café talk about the positive contributions of an activist taken too soon.

Later that evening, Julia was also able to put the case of Peridale's mysterious alien to bed, ridding

Evelyn of her guilt for possibly causing a man's stroke, thanks to a text from Nick: *Hey, not asking for my job back, just wanted to say I think my auntie came to see your husband saying an alien killed my uncle. Sorry about that. Tell the tarot card woman it wasn't her fault. My aunt's neighbour got a really bright light installed and it was the first time she'd seen it. Hope you've found the right person for the café.*

Easter Sunday was when Julia really felt things settle back into place, though the dust didn't quite land in the same place. Early that morning, before opening her café to the toddlers, she'd found herself crying and hugging her sister again – although for altogether more positive reasons.

"The hospital wants me to take the rest of the month off and go in for a review meeting," Sue had started, showing her nerves from the moment her lips parted; maybe the bottom lip wobble didn't just indicate lying. "There's a chance I'll get my job back in light of what happened with Sharon, and there's a chance I won't. Either way, I've decided – Neil and I have decided – that I'm going to take a year off from medicine to figure out where I fit."

"I think that's the best idea you've ever had. Find your passion again."

"It's not like the field ends at A&E," she'd said with a shaky laugh. "I kept trying to move away to the quieter wards, but the war stories kept dragging me back to the trenches. I think I'm just ready to go home, but I'm still going to need a job, so—"

"Sue, do you want to work here?" Julia couldn't stand the suspense. "I've been dying to ask you, but I sort of had a feeling *you* were going to ask, and—"

"Oh, thank heavens. I thought you might have found someone, and the idea of working part time around the corner from my house, my husband, and my girls is" – this is where the crying started – "it's all I've ever wanted."

Toddlers soon took over the café, ripping the place to shreds with their bare fists in search of the hundreds of mini-Easter eggs Julia had hidden around the place. Julia couldn't have been happier to be in her café on a Sunday with her new employee.

Julia's Café had always been a family affair, anyway. She said a silent 'thank you' to Melissa, glad she now had the opportunity to reach a hand to her sister one more time.

"Everyone's inside celebrating," Dot said when Barker joined her in looking at the ads in the post office window. "Wonderful news, isn't it? No Nick, Saskia, or

Melissa needed, just Sue. I suppose I can stop worrying about my granddaughter now."

Dot didn't sound so sure, so he asked, "Suppose?"

"It's nothing, it's just ..." Her eyes left the now-unnecessary ad for help in the café next door. "Well, we still don't know *how* Sue got that house, and she's told me to stop asking her, which I will, but ..." She sighed, shaking the thought away. "Doesn't matter now, does it? I'm sure everything will be absolutely fine with Sue from now on. Nothing to worry about."

"And *you*?"

Dot shot a sideways glance at him.

"What about me?"

"Still bored without your neighbourhood watch group?"

"Only boring people get bored, Barker. I live a *very* full life that consists of all the movement and bingo an old woman sliding towards the grave could want." She rolled a stone around under the tip of her shoe. "Why? Has Julia mentioned getting the band back together now that she's finally about to go part-time?"

Offering an apologetic smile, Barker shook his head.

"No, didn't think so," she said, mirroring his smile. "Ah, well. Something will come up. Maybe Percy will have us playing bowls or entering the dogs into a show or..."

"Or gardening at the allotment?" Barker produced a key and placed it straight into Dot's palm. "The spare for Plot Seven at Henderson. I'm not sure if I'm any readier for an allotment now than I was when I moved here, but given the waiting lists, I'd be a fool to hand it back. Before you take it, go to a locksmith and—"

"Copies, drawer, and trusted person, I know," she said, holding the key up as the Sunday sun started to fade for the day. "You know, Barker, occasionally you have something of an old woman about you. I'm sure Percy will be most pleased. He's rather enjoyed getting his hands stuck in."

Barker was glad to hear it, but he'd been hoping for more excitement from Dot.

"And you?"

Dot looked back to the post office window, her eyes going to a bright, colourful ad in the middle of the window. "I guess you could say I'm looking for more of an adventure. We should get back inside. That five-tier cake Julia whipped up for the occasion won't eat itself."

Dot left to rejoin the party, but Barker remained, already full of the double chocolate fudge layer he'd demolished a good portion of. He was over the moon that Julia had solved her staffing issue with Sue. And most importantly, that the case was over. He returned to his office under the café; he'd only left because he heard Dot say she was going for 'fresh air' before finding her at the post office.

Pulling in his chair behind his laptop, Barker finished writing up his case notes for the Henry Foreman case. He'd been to visit Coral twice since, and she'd updated him about Nadia. Coral had confirmed Sharon's story that Nadia had been about to leave with Henry the night of the launch and, to everyone's relief, confirmed that she was already in the process of divorcing Dr Khan, who hadn't been seen at the hospital since his release. There was already a FOR SALE sign outside of their house at Henderson Place, and as it turned out…

"She didn't even needs to work anyway," Coral had said when she'd topped Barker's plate up to the brim. "Inherited a chemist's empire from her father and solds it on years ago. Poor mite was absolutely loaded this whole time, so no wonder that man tried so hard to keep his boot on her neck. Said half the reason she took so many shifts was so she didn't have to go home. He trapped her in a cage; she just didn't realise she was the one holding the key. My Henry would have given her a better life … but we can't go back. Tell your wife this carrot cake is the best I've had, by the way. If the rest of her cakes are like this, I might venture out of this forest a little more often from now on. I think it's what Henry would have wanted."

Barker closed his laptop. It wasn't a perfect happy ending – few cases had those – but several people who deserved second chances were getting them. Henry hadn't been so lucky, but if Johnny's final tribute issue was anything to go by, he'd motivated enough people that his death was, ironically, the thing that would spread his inspiration just a little further.

All the way to Barker, too.

The Body at the Allotment would make a great third book.

But first, the time capsule – and he'd promised PC Puglisi he wouldn't 'take forever' finishing it.

Chapter Two...

Later that night, leaving the party in the dining room at Julia's cottage, Jessie followed Johnny into the hallway. Jessie couldn't have been more pleased that Sue was joining the café. Not just because it meant her life might finally calm down a little, but because it meant they could put a stop to their job hunt. She'd known from the start that her mum hadn't wanted anyone but family to work there, just like it had always been.

"My train's coming in shortly," Johnny said when they were at the door. "I'd rather just sneak out than say another goodbye."

"You'll be back soon," she said, giving him a hug. "Thanks for everything, Johnny. You really pushed me to that B."

"You did the work."

"I had a little help from life. Turns out, once you start thinking about Shakespeare, he's everywhere. I wonder if Sharon knew she was mirroring him when she poisoned Henry and stabbed Nadia?"

"Did Juliet know she was mirroring Romeo?" Johnny asked, chuckling as he pushed up his glasses. "Enough Shakespeare for now. There was one last thing I wanted to give you before I left." He reached into his messenger bag and pulled out a thick file. "You're going to need this."

"More coursework?"

"No, it's for the paper. Well, the stuff I *couldn't* print in the paper. It's my Greg Morgan file. I started following the money around the time of the library sell-out, and all roads kept leading back to our local MP. Wellington Heights, James Jacobson, the Crowd Pleaser Festival, and now Henderson Place. All these dodgy decisions leading to deaths, and nobody is looking at him. I sent a copy to the police, but I'm not sure what – if anything – they're doing with it."

"What do *I* do with it?" she asked, flipping it open. "Shouldn't you give this to the new editor?"

"I'll let *you* do that." Johnny opened the door wide and nodded across the lane into the night. A light was on in the cottage, and someone was moving about with a box. "Everyone's been so distracted by Sue's celebration that they haven't noticed their new neighbour has moved in. I daresay she's expecting you, and she'll be in a much better mood than the last time you saw her. You can blame me for that. Shouldn't have dangled the offer in front of her without an official go-ahead. She was always my first choice for the job, but they had other ideas. They came around to see that she might just be the perfect person for the job. I hear she already has an up-and-coming young reporter in mind for her first hire, too …" He winked as he pushed up his glasses. "I'll see you around, Jessie. Don't stand in your own way too much."

Promising she'd try not to as she weighed up the file, Jessie squinted into the dark. There was no mistaking the pair of familiar giant red glasses she spotted through the window across the lane...

∽

Thank you for reading, and don't forget to **RATE/REVIEW!**

The Peridale Cafe story continues in...

**BANANA BREAD AND BETRAYAL
Coming MARCH 28th 2023!**

You can pre-order the eBook on Amazon now!

Thank you for reading!

DON'T FORGET TO RATE AND REVIEW ON AMAZON

Reviews are more important than ever, so show your support for the series by rating and reviewing the book on Amazon! Reviews are **CRUCIAL** for the longevity of any series, and they're the best way to let authors know you want more! They help us reach more people! I appreciate any feedback, no matter how long or short. It's a great way of letting other cozy mystery fans know what you thought about the book.

Being an independent author means this is my livelihood, and *every review* really does make a **huge difference**. Reviews are the best way to support me so I can continue doing what I love, which is bringing you, the readers, more fun cozy adventures!

WANT TO BE KEPT UP TO DATE WITH AGATHA FROST RELEASES? *SIGN UP THE FREE NEWSLETTER!*

www.AgathaFrost.com

You can also follow **Agatha Frost** across social media. Search 'Agatha Frost' on:

Facebook
Twitter
Goodreads
Instagram

ALSO BY AGATHA FROST

Claire's Candles
1. Vanilla Bean Vengeance
2. Black Cherry Betrayal
3. Coconut Milk Casualty
4. Rose Petal Revenge
5. Fresh Linen Fraud
6. Toffee Apple Torment
7. Candy Cane Conspiracies

Peridale Cafe
1. Pancakes and Corpses
2. Lemonade and Lies
3. Doughnuts and Deception
4. Chocolate Cake and Chaos
5. Shortbread and Sorrow
6. Espresso and Evil
7. Macarons and Mayhem
8. Fruit Cake and Fear
9. Birthday Cake and Bodies
10. Gingerbread and Ghosts

11. Cupcakes and Casualties
12. Blueberry Muffins and Misfortune
13. Ice Cream and Incidents
14. Champagne and Catastrophes
15. Wedding Cake and Woes
16. Red Velvet and Revenge
17. Vegetables and Vengeance
18. Cheesecake and Confusion
19. Brownies and Bloodshed
20. Cocktails and Cowardice
21. Profiteroles and Poison
22. Scones and Scandal
23. Raspberry Lemonade and Ruin
24. Popcorn and Panic
25. Marshmallows and Memories
26. Carrot Cake and Concern
27. Banana Bread and Betrayal

Other

The Agatha Frost Winter Anthology

Peridale Cafe Book 1-10

Peridale Cafe Book 11-20

Claire's Candles Book 1-3

Printed in Great Britain
by Amazon